ALPHA MAGIC

HALLOWEEN WHYCHOOSE WITCHES
BOOK ONE

AMELIA SHAW

PROLOGUE

Halloween night. One year ago.

Our mothers said that three of us were Fated—blessed. What they actually meant was, I would be stuck with these two pain-in-the-ass best friends until my dying day.

"So, are we going to do this, or not?" I asked my friends, staring at each of them in turn. "Because there's no going back after this." My heart was pounding like a runaway train. If we didn't cast the spell now, I was afraid we'd never have the guts to do it.

The wind moved through the trees around us, rustling the leaves and signaling a fall storm was well on its way. We were gathered outside beneath the full moon, and the dark, starless sky, on a large, countryside property in the middle of nowhere. From here we couldn't be seen, so as long as we never said a word, no one would ever know about our little adventure or what we were up to on this sacred Halloween night; and our joint twenty-first birthday.

Tiffany, the blonde bombshell of our little group, nodded fiercely.

I could see the determination in her bright blue eyes.

She wanted this as much as I did.

I turned to Bella.

She had her teeth buried firmly in her lower lip.

I rolled my eyes. "Come on, Bella. You know we can't do this without you." And I meant that literally. Bella was a powerful witch and without her magic, I wasn't sure Tiff and I could pull off a spell of such magnitude.

She frowned and I could see the hesitation in the set of her shoulders and in the uncertain flicker of her dark brown gaze.

I narrowed my eyes at the girl who'd been practically a sister to me since the day we were born. "Come on, Bella. *Please.*"

We'd been talking about this spell for years, now, planning every part of the complex incantation. Waiting until the night we were old enough, powerful enough, and gutsy enough to pull it off.

Suddenly Bella's gaze hardened.

Relief poured through me. I knew that look. She was on my side now.

"Okay, Ruby. I'm in. Let's do this."

I grabbed my two best friends' hands, and they grabbed each other, forming a perfect triangle of strength. Our mothers were best friends, united in the abandonment by the fathers of their children. They'd made sure we grew up together, strong, bonded, and most of all, loyal to one another.

We clasped our hands and glanced down at the old book between us. I'd found it ten years ago, hidden in a stash of my mother's things. It was a powerful spell book that had once belonged to my late grandmother.

Without delay we began our chant, reciting the incantation in an ancient language lost to time and memory.

I closed my eyes and tried to relax, having memorized the spell years ago. I spoke my part and my friends spoke theirs. Each verse was a call to the magic that rippled in our veins—to Fate—and most of all, to the unconditional love that we all so desperately desired and craved.

Over and over, we chanted our words, our rhythm growing, while the magic in our blood, in our very ancestry, simmered, ready to burst at the seams.

I could feel the enchantment's mystical heat swell within me, building until sweat rolled down my face. I didn't stop. *I wouldn't.* And neither would Bella or Tiffany. The power of our combined magic swirled around us, alive and violent like a hurricane. I clung to the spell with all my might, focusing everything I had on this one moment. This spell would change our destinies. If we succeeded we'd never end up like our mothers—abandoned and alone.

I opened my eyes. The ancient book floated in the space between us.

Bella was watching the phenommenon with trepidation.

Tiff grinned when she caught my eye.

Bouyed on, we chanted louder, the words in our hearts building naturally as the spell came to a great crescendo.

I stared in awe at our joined hands, filled with excitement as a bright white light shone between our clenched fingers.

A sudden surge of power rippled between us, and the urge to finish the spell gripped me with a sense of urgency. I nodded at my honorary sisters and together we forged on with the spell. There was no going back now. As we uttered the final words, the white magic we'd conjured shot into the air above our heads with a cosmic *boom*, exploding in a spectacular eruption of color, like fireworks sparkling against the dark night sky.

The impact of the explosion blew us back with surprising force, each of us landing awkwardly with a *thump* on the dewy grass.

I groaned as I rolled onto my side to relieve the pressure on the bruised flesh of my backside, quickly looking back to the sky as the magic sprayed outward like a wave, then seemed to disappear. A small measure of disappointment hit me square in the chest. I'd expected more than some magical fireworks, followed by an unsatisfying dissipation. Though what I'd actually thought might happen, I couldn't really say.

Silence enveloped the night once more in the wake of our All Hallows' Eve casting. The stars shimmered, the trees swayed in the breeze, and the moonlight shone down on a gorgeous country house a long way off in the distance.

"Is that it?" I asked.

As though in answer, the spell book that had been hovering in the air, dropped and landed in the dirt between us. The front cover closed by itself, all signs of magic, gone.

Tiffany stood first, brushing the dirt from her tight pants and groaning as though annoyed by the mess.

Bella and I got to our feet too, the anticipation and build-up finally beginning to leach the strength from me.

It was over. It was done. Now, all we had to do was wait for the spell to come to fruition. For the men—our men—to seek us out.

And patience, although a virtue, was definitely not one of my strengths. "So... back to the house for a celebratory drink?" I suggested, forcing some upbeat excitement into my tone.

We'd brought some alcohol with us, so why wouldn't we? Especially as we could finally *legally* drink in the human world.

"Sounds like a plan," Tiffany said with a flick of her long, blonde hair.

Then together we turned and trekked back to the house that Bella's family owned.

I glanced down at my hands, expecting something to have changed—anything. But as I glanced at each of my friends, it seemed that nothing was different for any of us. At least not physically, anyway.

I wondered if our loves, wherever they were, had been struck by our magic. Could they feel it, even now? Were they maybe already searching for us?

Once inside the little house in the woods, we flicked on the lights and used our magic to mix up cocktails with the colors of the sunset—red, orange, yellow, and a splash of dusky purple.

"Perfect." I raised my glass from the counter.

Tiffany and Bella plucked up their drinks as well, lifting their glasses to clink with mine.

"Happy birthday, ladies," I said, and they chorused the cheerful sentiment back to me. Sharing a birthday with my two best friends had been trying at times, especially growing up. I'd never had a party of my own, or a single day where I felt special just for being me. But now that we were grown and my more selfish childhood tendencies had dissolved into a real sense of sisterhood, I loved it.

We all took a sip of our first legal drink and mutually grimaced at the sheer amount of liquor I'd poured in the mix.

"Wow, that's strong," Tiff said, blinking rapidly as the vapours burned her eyes.

I nodded ruefully, swallowing hard as the vodka and gin cocktail blazed down my throat.

Bella gulped awkwardly, coughing and shuddering before she set the drink back down firmly on the counter. She waved her hand over the table in front of us and conjured us up a whole feast of savory and sweet snacks to celebrate. Chips, chocolate cake, cookies, and crackers with cheese littered the surface in front of us.

She was the best at making food. Actually, truth be told, she was the best at everything when it came to magic. But luckily for us, as the most introverted of our little trio, she never big noted herself or threw it in our faces.

"Oh, perfect. Thanks, Belle!" I grabbed some chips and stuffed them in my mouth without shame. I hadn't eaten dinner. I couldn't, not with all the nerves surrounding tonight's activities.

Bella sighed.

I glanced up at her, raising my eyebrows in question. It was obvious she wanted to say something.

"What's up Bell-Bell?"

"Do you think it worked?" she asked, giving voice to the question we were all thinking about, and all wanted answered.

I shrugged, forcing myself to appear nonchalant, though I was anything but. This spell would hopefully change the course of all our lives for the better. I gave her the only answer I could. "I don't know. I hope so. I mean, I guess we'll find out."

"I hope so, too!" Tiffany said, her tone exasperated. "We've only been planning this since forever."

I conjured up some stools for us and we all sat down around our tasty birthday spread.

We chatted and ate, drank and laughed, celebrating our whole lives ahead of us.

All through the night I hoped that our magic was working its way to the men for whom we were destined, because the spell we had woven together tonight was a spell that called out to Fate, itself for our one, true love.

Our mothers had been abandoned before we were even born. We'd grown up surrounded by sorrow, loneliness, and heartache. None of us wanted that for ourselves or any future children we might have. Finding the perfect match was clearly a game of Russian Roulette, and we weren't taking any chances!

That's why tonight, we'd sent out a call for the men who would love us for all eternity. Our perfect matches. The men who would stand by us, love us, and never leave us. We wanted them to manifest in our lives quickly of course, but they would answer the call of Fate when they were good and ready. Or at least, that's what I assumed.

Whether that would be tomorrow, next month, or next year— I would wait. And I knew Bella and Tiffany would, too. Because only Fate could be trusted with such an important a decision as the person we were meant to spend the rest of our lives with.

Born to three single mothers, not a father between us, we certainly had trust issues aplenty. I, for one, wasn't going to date just anyone. And I definitely wasn't going to fall in love with the first guy who happened to look my way and smile. I'd rather be alone forever than live with the pain my mother wore upon her shoulders like a heavy coat of sorrow.

So, with any luck, Fate would conspire with our magic and wouldn't let us down. We'd risked everything, tonight, to ensure that our futures would unfold in a drastically different way to our mothers'.

CHAPTER 1
RUBY

One year later.

My day job at the local florist certainly wasn't glamorous, but it passed the time all the same. "Have a nice day," I said to the human woman who'd just bought a bunch of beautiful roses for her sick mother. I waved her out the door. What I really should have done was tuck in a spell for her mother's flu, but we were forbidden to do magic around the humans in town.

I let out a huge sigh and looked around the large shop filled with neat buckets of brightly colored flowers and lush potted plants. What was I doing here again?

"Making yourself useful until you work out what you want to do with your life", my mother's voice sounded in my head.

The witches in my family were healers, fortune tellers, and teachers. But unlike all the women who had come before me, I had no idea what I wanted to do with my lifet. I'd graduated high school with good grades, gone to community college, then... nothing. I was adrift, but that wasn't my personality generally speaking. I wasn't a flake. But unlike so many of those within the witching community who were addicted to the coven lifestyle, I just... wasn't.

I wasn't even sure if I wanted to hang around this town forever. Travel sounded more interesting to me; the chance to really see the world. If only I could convince Bella and Tiffany to come along.

"Ruby, I'm just heading out to the bank. Do you want me to grab anything for lunch?" Andrea, my boss, smiled at me as she picked up her handbag from behind the counter and headed to the front door.

"No. I'm all good today. Thanks, Andrea." I smiled at her as she left.

Such a lovely woman, especially for a human.

When my mother had realized I couldn't make up my mind about what I wanted to do with my life, she'd forced me to get a job with a non-magical person. To learn, to expand my horizons, and to be of use to the community. Which, at the time, I'd thought was a horrible idea. But as it turned out, there were a lot of nice humans here. It really wasn't so bad.

The school I'd attended had been mostly for witches, and I'd kept my head down at college and mostly associated with those I knew. Again, mostly witches. Now, it was kind of nice to be able to weave between the different communities; not that the humans knew what I was, of course.

I turned back to the flowers I'd been artfully arranging when my last customer had come in. A phone order had come through for a large bunch of white lilies and sweet violets. Simple, but lovely. I was so tempted to use my magic to make them brighter, bigger, and even more spectacular. But the consequences for revealing magic to the non-magicals was far too severe to risk.

So, instead, I focused on my more artistic skills. I arranged them in a nice bunch, wrapping paper and plastic around the stems, before tying it off with a large orange ribbon to contrast with the vivid purple of the violets.

The bell above the door tinkled, alerting me to a new customer.

"With you in a moment," I called over my shoulder toward the front door. An unexpected tingle of awareness shot up my spine like sizzling electricity. I shivered, not with cold but with the feeling of impending change. My breath caught in my throat as I twisted around to see who had set off such a drastic shift in the world around me.

A huge man stood in the shop, staring at me with quiet intensity.

His rugged beauty struck me like a slap to the face. Soulful, dark blue eyes regarded me, while brown locks fell to his shoulders. His features were so stunning it made me want to crawl over the counter and jump right into his arms. The only thing that stopped me in my tracks was the fact that the striking man standing before me who was staring at me like he'd never even seen a woman before, wasn't *just* a man. I took a deep breath through my nose and shivered at the gruff, animalistic notes.

He was a shifter, but not just any shifter. He was a wolf, and not just any damn wolf, but an Alpha.

I'd come across one once by accident when I was a child in the forest. The scent of an Alpha was like barely leashed power, earthy sweat, and a strong animal musk. I'd never forgotten the way I'd felt that day, and now I was standing before another one—this time in human form.

I placed my hands on the counter in front of me, digging my nails into the wood, grounding myself. I didn't want to embarrass myself by squealing or screaming. But it was incredibly hard to remain calm in the face of laying eyes upon who I felt was surely my one true love... the one the spell had summoned. I cleared my throat with a cough and forced myself to lsmile up at him. "Hi, can I help you?"

His beauty was intoxicating, and if he wasn't something like six feet six, well, I'd bite my own bum!

"You're a witch," he said. It was a statement. Not a question.

"Shh..." I said, hushing him as my brow furrowed. "You're lucky my boss has ducked out to the bank."

He frowned. "She doesn't know?"

"We don't tell humans what we are. You know that." I crossed my arms over my chest and quirked my brow at him. "Do you go around shouting to them that you're an Alpha wolf shifter?"

His eyes went wide and he stared at me with his mouth open, an expression of shock written all over his face. He looked as if I'd just hit him over the head with a frying pan.

"What's wrong? Cat got your tongue?" I asked, grinning at him for several long moments. *Damn, he's beautiful. So beautiful.* Though that was probably the wrong word to describe his appearance. His jawline was darkened with the beginnings of a new beard, and the muscles bulging under the gray hoodie he wore hinted at an incredibly lethal body. Hot... that's what he was. *Damn HOT.*

"But what are you, exactly?" he asked. It sounded almost like an accusation.

"What do you mean, what am I?" I repeated and frowned at him. He knew I was a witch. What more did he want? "I'm Ruby. Why are you here? What's wrong?"

"How did you know *that* about me?" he asked, his tone growly. "I'm not the Alpha... not yet, anyway."

"But it's in your blood, isn't it?" I asked, second-guessing myself now. I couldn't be wrong about that, could I? The other Alpha I'd met was in wolf form.

He took a few steps forward, his intense blue gaze focused on me. "Yes, it is. So, answer my question. How'd you know that?"

My breath caught in my throat the closer he moved, the scent of him seemed so familiar, like a long-forgotten memory. But how was that possible? I'd never met him before in my life. I was sure of it.

"I..." I swallowed and dropped my arms, grabbing for the counter again as my knees threatened to buckle beneath me. "I met an Alpha wolf when I was child. He smelled the same as you," I explained.

The Alpha crept closer, until he stood right in front of the counter I was leaning on for support.

I had to tilt my head up to look into his eyes, and when I did, a noise slipped from my mouth. One that I couldn't decipher. Was it a moan? A prayer? A curse? *What is going on?* I gripped the counter more desperately as my trembling legs finally gave way. This was going to hurt if I didn't save myself—and fast.

I muttered a spell and conjured a chair beneath me. I fell into it, feeling as intoxicated as I assumed being drunk felt like. Witches had a great natural resistance to alcohol, like most para-normals, so I'd never felt what being tipsy was actually like, let alone been fully intoxicated. But I had to assume it felt something like this strange, hot, tingly feeling that pulsed through my veins, making me weak at the knees, weepy, and ridiculously and inexplicably aroused.

Damn, that's what this is! Arousal. Heat pulsated from my core, radiating through my belly and down my still trembling legs. I forced myself to look up at him, and he was staring at me as though he were waiting for something. "Um..." My brain had gone frustratingly blank. "Um, sorry, did you ask me another question?"

He shook his head and growled a little, swallowing and coughing as though he suddenly couldn't speak.

What was going on? The bell tinkled again over the front door and Andrea strolled back in. I jumped to my feet and made my chair vanish before she saw it.

"Welcome back," I greeted her, putting on my cheeriest smile and happiest voice, though inside my head, my world was positively spinning.

This guy... this wolf shifter... he had to be my soul mate. The one I'd called for on Halloween last year. *Didn't he?* Nothing else made sense. He was so much hotter, bigger, and older than I'd imagined. But I'd never expected a wolf shifter. *Damn.* How was my mom going to take this news?

Andrea placed her black handbag on the counter and frowned at the Alpha wolf in front of me. "Can I help you?" she ask rather brusquely.

I was surprised by her non-welcoming response, especially coming from one of the friendliest women I'd ever met. Didn't she feel his strength, his power? How wasn't she affected by his otherworldly beauty? Then something my mother had once told me swam up into my subconscious. *"Humans don't like shifters."* Wolves, especially. They could feel the danger in them, which to us, was an aphrodisiac. However, for a human, it just smelled like trouble.

And boy, am I in trouble...

The guy nodded at Andrea and pushed a piece of paper across the desk at us.

I glanced down at it. It was an order for a bouquet of lilies and violets.

"Oh, these are for you, sir!" I squeaked in my nervousness to diffuse the situation. I didn't want Andrea showing any aggression at him. He wasn't doing anything wrong—not yet anyway.

I twisted around, grabbed the flowers I'd just finished arranging, and turned back to him in a hurry. I leaned over the counter and offered the bouquet to the huge man, even though I felt pretty certain they were meant to be mine.

"Thank you," he managed to say, though he sounded garbled, and his teeth were unusually pointed as he forced the words out. Almost... wolf-like. His teeth hadn't looked like that when he'd first come into the shop. He pulled out a credit card from his wallet.

I glanced down at the name before sliding it through the sensor on the side of the register monitor. I couldn't help myself.

Jackson Davis.

Oh, I liked the sound of that. But where did he live? Where was he from? Was he just passing through town or did he belong to a local pack? *I have to find out!* I processed his payment and handed back his plastic.

He plucked the card from my hand with his fingertips, careful not to touch me as he took it.

A flush of disappointment washed over me. I ached to touch him, to see if I could feel something tangible and physical between us. It was still early days in my training as a witch, but all my teachers had always said that I had a natural affinity for scrying and future predictions; that my instincts were always right on target. And every instinct, every vibe, and every ounce of my witchy genes was telling me that Jackson and I would be seeing *a lot* more of each other in the future.

"Thank you," he mumbled again as he backed away, though he barely opened his mouth to speak this time.

I cocked my head at him and watched as he turned on his his heels to leave. What was with the weird talking thing? Or more precisely, the lack of talking?

Was he fighting the urge to shift? Did he feel the attraction between us that radiated as bright and brilliant as the noonday sun? I wanted to know so badly what was going on inside that beautiful head of his.

"Oh, ah..." I tried to call out to him as he left, but he strode for the door as if in a hurry. The bells clanged unceremoniously as he all but launched himself outside.

I stared at him through the window as he climbed up into his truck and high-tailed it out of his parking spot in front of the shop before I even had the time to walk around the counter.

Andrea shook her head and *tsked* loudly as she opened the cash register and began unloading the change she'd gotten from the bank. "He sounded like such a nice man over the phone. I'm sorry you had to wait on him while I was out. I'm sure he scared you."

"Scared me?" I repeated, moving away from Andrea to arrange some nearby roses. Idle hands... devil's work, and all that.

"Oh, yes," Andrea said, shuddering. "Didn't he bother you? The size of him... the feel of him. Ugh." She shuddered again.

I clenched my jaw, feeling surprisingly defensive. Why couldn't she see that there was nothing wrong with him? That instead, something wrong with her? I swallowed down my sudden anger. It was for the good of all humanity that they were afraid of the shifters. It was natural. And I shouldn't allow myself to be offended—even though my face was flushed with heat, and latent rage simmered away inside me.

It's a good thing. It's a good thing. Don't get mad. I repeated over and over. I faced the roses I was toying with so she couldn't see my reddening face and forced myself to continue with a completely normal and casual turn of conversation. "Who were the flowers for, do you know? His wife, maybe? Did he say?" There hadn't been a card ordered, so I was left hoping someone hadn't snagged him before I could.

"His grandmother, I think," Andrea said absently as she went into the back to check stock.

I was left staring out the window. Was this the man I was meant to love? The one that our Halloween spell had called upon? Everything in me said *yes*.

But none of us had so much as even had a single date since that fateful night on All Hallows' Eve exactly twelve months ago. But from the feel of Jackson Davis and the prickling hairs at the nape of my neck, I was pretty sure I'd just met my *one*. My only. My soulmate.

And he was a wolf shifter. *Damn. I hope the coven doesn't mind!*

CHAPTER 2

JACKSON

"What the fuck was that?!" I growled at myself from the inside my truck cabin, slamming the palm of my hand over and over on the steering wheel.

Thump. Thump. Thump.

My skin was on fire, my wolf shifter leaping within my gut to break free. He wanted to rip through me and roar to the sky that he'd found his mate. *No!* No, it couldn't be. She's not a shifter! She wasn't even a human! And I wasn't ready to find my mate yet. I was barely twenty-eight! I wanted more time to travel, to explore, to be free.

If she'd been a shifter, *maybe* I'd be able to wrap my head around the fact I'd just found my mate. It would have been fine, and ideal long-term, actually. But she wasn't even human, which would have been inferior, but at least accepted within my pack. A witch, though? *Hell, no.* Our children would be some strange, terrible half-breeds. *Don't overreact*, I chastised myself.

Exhaling sharply, all the fight went out of me as I slumped in my seat. "Just focus on the road, you idiot."

A large part of me—namely the sane, non-wolf part—was screaming that it couldn't be true. Just couldn't be. That part— my more human part—said that this was some weird mix-up and that my shifter was just horny or something. *Though she had the scent of an innocent...*

"Damn it!" I slammed my clenched fist into the steering wheel, hard this time.

A witch and a virgin as well? She'd probably blow my damn head off the first time we had sex. What was Fate up to now? Because she was seriously screwing with me. With a sigh I turned right off Main Street and followed the road around to my grand-mother's house; the only human relative I had.

My brothers never visited her, but she'd been a good and stable influence in my life since I was a child and I wasn't inter-ested in shunning her. And no one else had, until Grandpa had died. Weird how that had changed everything. I parked my truck in her driveway and turned off the engine. "Wonder what she'll think about this twist?"

The front door opened, and Grandma stepped out onto the porch, waving at me with a huge, welcoming smile on her face.

I sighed heavily and grabbed the flowers, which still smelled vaguely of my mate's touch. I grimaced as I hopped out of the truck. Her scent had me hardening like a pond in winter. I needed to think cool thoughts, and fast.

"Jackson! What brings you here?" Grandma called out as I rounded the truck and headed toward her. Her long, gray hair was piled on top of her head in a large, round bun, and she was looking paler than normal.

I frowned as I approached. "Hey Grandma, Mom said you weren't feeling so good."

"Pah," Grandma said, swatting at the air as though there was a fly nearby "I'm fine."

I lifted the flowers and offered them to her.

She sighed and made a huffing noise at the same time. "You shouldn't have," she said, but she smiled as she took them and leaned down to smell them. "Thank you."

I waited patiently.

Finally she waved me inside. "Oh, come in, come in."

We strolled inside, away from the sounds of the humans next door, and I could relax a little. There was something about town that always set me on edge, and now I had an extra reason for it.

"Let me get us some lemonade. I even made an orange cake this morning," Grandma said as she gesture toward the large couch in her sitting room. "Sit, sit."

I grinned as I collapsed onto the couch.

She toddled off to grab whatever treats she had created.

There was nothing like homemade baked goods. They soothed the soul.

When she came back into the room, she put the flowers that were now in a vase on the table. But the best part was that she also returned with a plate of desserts the size of my broad chest.

"Ah, expecting guests?" I asked, quirking my brow at the mound of cake and chocolate chip cookies.

She poured me a glass of homemade lemonade. "Well, it's Halloween tomorrow," she said, as though that answered the question.

"And…?" I asked, before shoving a chocolate chip cookie into my mouth, groaning as the chocolate melted on my tongue. *Just out of the oven. Perfect.*

"And I like to give the little trick-or-treaters a homemade treat. None of that town-bought candy rubbish," she said, shaking her head as though the tradition of hoarding candy in a bag for months after Halloween was a bad thing.

I chuckled. "Well, you do go all out. These cookies are amazing." I grabbed another one then picked up the glass of lemonade she'd poured. "Thank you, this is great."

Grandma leaned back on her sofa and narrowed her eyes at me. "What's going on, Jackson? You don't seem quite like yourself."

I tried to smile, but it came out as more of a grimace. "Just came to see you." Which was true, I had initially.

"Mmhmm…" she hummed, giving me the eye that meant she didn't believe me.

I sighed. "I *did*. I had the day off work and Mom said you hadn't been well, and I realized that I've been slack in seeing you."

"Then what happened?" she asked, raising one eyebrow.

"I… ordered flowers from a florist in town. Just to, you know, apologize for not coming to visit more often."

She nodded sagely. "Yes. Then what happened to make you so antsy?"

I grabbed another cookie. This was another reason I loved my grandmother. She read me better than anyone else in the family. It was confrontational sometimes, but it was reassuring to know that someone loved me enough to check in on me and see how I was really doing.

I swallowed hard, my tongue thick and my throat tight. God, this was more difficult to say than I'd expected. "The girl who works at the florist..."

"The new girl? With the gorgeous red hair? I'm not sure of her name," my grandmother mused, her eyes lighting up with interest.

I shook my head. "I don't know it, either." I hadn't looked, hadn't wanted to know. If she'd been wearing a name tag, I didn't see it.

"So? What about her?" my grandmother probed.

"I think..." I clenched my jaw, forcing myself to say it. *Come on, Jackson! You're from a fucking Alpha bloodline. Pull your shit together.* I cleared my throat roughly and tried again. "No... I mean, *I know,* she's my mate."

My grandmother clapped her hands together, bouncing softly on the couch in her excitement. "Oh, Jackson, darling. That's wonderful!"

I scowled at her unintentionally. "It is not. She's a witch, Grandma. Did you know that?"

"Pah," my grandmother said, waving her hand to dismiss my agitation. "So what? In this town, everyone's *something.*"

That wasn't true. Most of the town's people were human.

"But she's not a shifter! Don't you understand what that means?"

My grandmother nodded. "Yes. Instead of turning into a wolf whenever she wants, she'll be able to work magic every day of her life and probably make me some absolutely kickass great grandbabies."

I put my empty glass down and collapsed against the sofa back. "You don't get it, not my long shot, Grandma."

She sighed. "Of course, I get it. Why do you think I live in town rather than being closer to my kids, and grandkids?"

I shrugged. "No idea." I hadn't really ever thought about it. I mean, I'd wondered about it a few times. Like, why had she moved away from us after our grandfather died? I'd assumed at the time that it was to be close to her human friends. For support or... something. I ran a hand through my disheveled hair in annoyance.

She picked up a cookie and inspected it. "It's because your pack is full of speciesist *assholes.* Despite all the years I'd lived with the pack, they made me feel wholly unwelcome after your grandfather passed. All because I'm human—even though I was family."

"Speciesist?" I repeated. Was she serious?

She laughed at me. "Why do you look so shocked? You're a prime example of it, yourself."

"Me?" I repeated. I'd never been called such a thing in my life.

"Yes, you." She narrowed her gaze at me, though there was very little heat in the look. "Just look at you, all horrified that Fate dared to send you a beautiful young girl as your mate! You're all twisted up simply because she's not a wolf shifter. Well, I'll be the first oen to say it. I'm glad she's not! That pack has become far too inbred. Look at the lack of females being born, if at all. Look at the infertility of your generation." Grandma shook her head in dismay.

"The..." *What?*

I hadn't even thought about it. We were lacking in females. *Yes... I suppose we were.* Not that I had any issues finding a nightly bed warmer if I needed or wanted one. There were a dozen packs within an hour's drive, and there were willing women in all of them.

But Grandma was right. There weren't many females that were available to mate with. I'd heard my father say it once. That in the past twenty years there hadn't been a single pack female born. But it hadn't concerned me. After all, there were other packs. Other shifters. Why should I care? And now that I thought about it, there were very few babies being born in general. I hadn't even seen a pregnant woman in... I don't know how many years.

She nodded slowly. "You need to talk to some of your friends, and your parents, too, Jackson. That pack is in trouble, and if you ignore this call from Fate, you may end up like half the other men in your pack—alone and childless."

"That won't happen," I said, sitting up straight. I was Alpha born. No female shifter in her right mind would deny me. "Not that I'm ready for that kind of committment, anyway."

Grandma rolled her eyes at me. "Oh, cut out the Peter Pan shit. You're twenty-eight years old. Your father was twenty-five when he married your mother, and your grandfather was barely twenty-one when we were married. I'm surprised it's taken you this long to find her."

I rolled my eyes. "Come on, Grandma. That's not fair."

"What's not fair is that you've gotten away with being rootless this long. It's time, obviously, or Fate wouldn't have sent you this girl. Now, forget all the crap you've been taught—that you *must* mate with a shifter." She rolled her eyes for emphasis. "You wouldn't exist if your grandfather had ignored the pull of Fate and decided not to marry me."

I nodded slowly, dumbstruck. "That's true."

Even as a pure human, my grandmother had produced five strong sons for my grandfather. All excellent fighters. There was obviously nothing wrong with mating outside of our pack, I'd just never expected the need.

My heart suddenly swelled, and happiness pulsed along my veins. "Thanks, Grandma."

She nodded. "You're welcome. Now, have some cake." She shoved the plate at me, and we went back to less heated subjects.

On the way home I was left with a strange feeling in my gut, which was odd as my grandmother's words had me rethinking all of my pre-conceived notions about with whom I'd mate and when. She was right. Fate always knew best. But still, something was wrong. There was something missing. I just wasn't sure what it was.

CHAPTER 3

DARREN

My grandmother had been a full blood witch, one of the few accepted by pack men in the past. She'd died a few years ago but throughout my life it had become obvious that I'd inherited a few of her traits. An uncomfortable ability to know when something was wrong was one of those things.

I spotted the guy I was looking for as he walked out the front door of his parents' house. I called out, "Hey, Billy. I need to speak to Jackson. Do you know where he went?"

Billy, who was Jackson's cousin, stopped in his tracks to answer me. "Yeah, I heard he went to the florist in town to pick up some stuff for Grandma, then was going to see her."

I nodded, tension eating at my gut.

"I need to go find him," I said, knowing full well what Billy would say next.

He stared at me for a minute, then shrugged. "Sure. I'll come with you. Haven't seen Grandma in ages, anyway. Wanna take my truck?"

"Yeah. Thanks."

Billy had the better vehicle between us, a black truck with a bull bar and massive wheels. Not my style, but it was definitely comfortable.

Once we jumped into the truck, he turned to me. "You sure you don't wanna wait until he gets home? He probably won't be long."

I opened the door and shook my head. "Nah. I've got to find him now."

Billy shrugged but didn't argue, settling into his seat in the cab alongside me. "Okay."

Most of the pack ignored my heritage, but they also did what I asked when I asked for it, irrespective of how weird it sounded at the time. They knew I had some strange insights and just went with it. We drove the fifteen minutes into town, looking out for Jackson's truck along the way. As we slowed down for the traffic on Main Street, the florist caught my eye.

A tingle unlike anything I'd ever felt passed over my neck. It felt like a warning, yet there was something positive and good behind the feeling as well. Something I shouldn't ignore, perhaps. "Hey. Stop there." I pointed.

"Where?" Billy asked, slowing down regardless of the fact he didn't know which way I meant.

I pointed toward the front window. "The flower shop! There. The store with the pink sign."

Billy pulled hard on the wheel and we turned straight across the road and parked outside the florist.

Billy glanced at me, a puzzled look on his face. "Yeah, I don't think Jackson will still be here."

"Probably not, but I.... want to go in. Just for a minute." I stepped out of the truck, surprised to see Billy getting out too. "You don't have to come," I told him, another strange sensory premonition passing over my skin. Something was about to happen.

He shrugged. "May as well buy something too. Can't have Jackson showing me up."

I had a retort for that but bit my tongue. Jackson and Billy, and most of their siblings, had practically abandoned their grandmother when she'd moved into town. I'd always wondered why. Other than the fact she was human, of course. But that shouldn't have been a reason to ignore the woman who had cared for them practically their whole lives. However, the pack was weird like that.

I pushed on the glass door as we entered the shop, the tinkle of a bell sounding above our head.

An older woman with dark hair and a cheery smile greeted us as we walked inside. "Hello. Can I help you?"

I smiled back at her, but soon recognized that this person wasn't the reason that I'd been called to come into the shop, but I responded to her just the same. "Yes, you can hopefully. I was just looking for a friend that came this way today. Jackson—"

Billy sidled up next to me and said in a low voice, "Hey, can you smell that?"

Being part witch rather than full shifter meant that my wolf senses weren't as attuned as his. Especially my sense of smell. "No. What do you..." Then I did smell it. A sexy, sweet, all-consuming scent that made me want to go down on my knees and thank the heavens for the person it belonged to. "Who?"

We both looked around the room. It couldn't be the old lady. There had to be someone else.

"Did you say Jackson?" came a voice from the right.

We both turned to stare at the angel who was walking through a staff-only door, toward us.

She had long, red hair and the most beautiful face. I'd never seen anyone so perfect, not even in my dreams.

My heart thumped in my chest as my mouth ran dry. Who was this magnificent creature and why was Billy growling beside me?

I forced myself to swallow and answer her question. "Ah, yes. He was headed this way and we stopped by to see if he was still here." Then it hit me with the force of a tornado. The knowledge. A fact. An irrefutable truth... She was a witch. And she was *my* Fated Mate. My knees trembled and I willed them to lock. If there'd been something nearby to grab, I would have hauled myself over to it.

"And you are?" I managed to say, glancing to my left.

Billy was shivering like he was freezing cold.

What is his problem?

She swallowed visibly, her eyes growing as round as the full moon.

I could see her magic pulsing like a silver halo radiating all around her.

"I... ah... Ruby. I'm Ruby."

"Ruby." I couldn't stop myself from repeating her name. It suited her, from her glowing red hair to the precious, beautiful jewel she obviously was.

"I'm Darren," I said. "And this is Billy."

Billy growled a little then snapped his jaw shut.

She stepped closer, biting her lip in a way that made me ache to kiss her. "Did you say you were looking for Jackson?"

"Yeah, why?"

Her cheeks warmed in a strange way, as though blushing at the mere mention of his name. "He came in to pick up some flowers, then left. He didn't say much."

I glanced over at Billy. It seemed like he was having the same trouble. I looked back to her, smiling broadly. "Do you always have that effect on men?"

She shook her head. "No! Oh my God. Not at all." She glanced away as though embarrassed.

Billy tugged on my jacket, pulling me toward the front door once again.

I didn't want to leave, but I could feel Billy's anxiety and need to get away. I chuckled and indicated to Billy with my thumb. "Ah… looks like I need to go, but I hope I'll see you again."

She nodded. "It's Halloween tomorrow night. I'll be around." She smiled brightly and there was a hint of understanding in her eyes.

Could she sense the witch in me also?

"Will you come back for All Hallows' Eve?"

Normally I wouldn't venture into town on Halloween, not even if someone paid me.

Billy continued to tug on my jacket.

"Definitely. See you then," I called back, following Billy outside, a laugh escaping me.

Billy ran straight for the truck like his life depended on it.

"Hey. What's going on with you?" I asked him. Then out of the corner of my eye, I saw Jackson in his black truck fly by. I nodded toward the retreating vehicle. "There's Jackson. Looks like we missed your grandmother's meeting. You still want to see her or go back to the pack?"

Billy paced the pavement by the truck like a man possessed, his hands clenching and unclenching. "The pack. Now," Billy managed to get out, before twisting around to jump in the truck.

I shrugged and followed his lead, then we took off after Jackson.

Billy was shaking like a dog trying to get water out of his coat, and he kept clenching his hands around the steering wheel as though he was attempting to wring the very life out of the poor truck.

"What's going on, Billy?" I asked casually, glancing hesitantly at the speedometer and hoping there weren't any cops nearby.

He was way over the limit, and we were catching Jackson fast.

I glanced ahead and pointed out the obvious. "Look. There's Jackson. You can slow down now," I said, injecting my tone with light-hearted laughter, hoping it would relax the wolf shifter beside me.

Billy didn't say anything, but he took his foot off the gas so that we were following Jackson at a safer and much more legal pace. He didn't even try and speak to me for the rest of the trip.

So, I just sat back and enjoyed the strange new feelings flowing through me. Now that I wasn't so focused on Billy and his weirdness, I could daydream about the glorious fact that I'd just found my mate. She wasn't a wolf, and she wasn't a human. She was a witch! How perfect was that? For me, anyway.

I'd always secretly wished I had more power than the small amount of intuition and fortune-telling I was gifted with. Of course, having Ruby as my wife wouldn't increase my own power, but our children would be *incredible*. Also, it would be a joy to see Ruby come into more of her power as she got older. She only looked to be about twenty-one, twenty-two, maybe. Most witches had only just started to develop their skills by that age. But this way, I would be there to see it all.

My dad wouldn't be thrilled about my news, but Mom

wouldn't mind. After all, it was her mother who was the full blood witch in the family.

The truck slowed down as we headed into our borough. Our pack had built the houses and roads a century ago, beginning with a large farm that had just a few houses on it, it had increased to a substantial settlement now. Though we relied on the town for most of our needs, we did grow some food and had our own local tradesmen. I, myself, was a sparky—one of about five electricians in the pack.

Billy pulled his truck up behind Jackson's, who had parked in the driveway in front of his house.

Most of us single guys still lived with our parents, or in bachelor housing set up for the extra males our pack seemed to be having.

Jackson was one of the few single men in the pack who'd already built his own house, but then again, he was a proverbial jack of all trades. He did construction, plastering, some plumbing, as well as brick laying. And to top it all off, he was an Alpha wolf, one of the few we had in our current generation. They were born and bred to lead by example and step up in times of stress and uncertainty. Luckily, we hadn't fought a battle or a decent enemy in decades, so Jackson could relax and just be another member of the pack.

Billy turned off the engine and jumped out.

I followed suit, a strong sense of contentment making my limbs feel warm and relaxed. I casually strode after Billy as he went straight for his cousin.

Jackson was just opening the front door to his house and called over his shoulder, "Hey, Billy. Come on in. Boy, do I have news for you."

"Hey," I said, lifting my hand and waving at him.

Jackson smiled at me in return, though he tilted his head curiously, as though confused as to why I was there.

I jumped in to explain, "I, ah,had a... premonition that I needed to find you. So Billy and I went into town to look for you."

"Oh." Jackson frowned, then like most people in the pack, just shrugged and went with it. "Okay. Come in, then." He waved us inside.

We stepped into the large living area and I couldn't stop myself from having a look around. I hadn't seen inside the house since it was finished. It was really impressive, with natural exposed beams and a large, open plan kitchen.

"Jackson, you won't fucking believe it!" Billy said, running his hand agitatedly through his hair.

"What?"

"I met my mate," Billy spat, as though it were the worst thing he'd ever admitted to.

Then it kicked me square in the balls. I spun back to face him. "What are you talking about?" He couldn't possibly be talking about *my* mate, could he? Because I was pretty sure that wasn't how all this worked.

Jackson chuckled, heading to the fridge. He opened the door and pulled out a six-pack of beer. "You guys want one?"

"Hell, yes," Billy said.

I didn't usually drink, but my instincts were telling me that today was going to be one of those rare times I did. "Yeah. Thanks."

Jackson cracked three of the cans and handed them over. "Well, it looks like it's the day for finding mates," he announced, puffing up his chest as though he was about to say something important. "Because I found mine, too."

I shuddered, an overwhelming sense of destiny shivering down my nerves and through my gut. "Fuck," I swore, as I shivered again. I gripped my beer tightly as I grabbed a nearby kitchen stool and pulled it abruptly towards me. I fell onto it, my legs giving way. This was *bad*. So very, very bad.

"You okay?" Billy asked from beside me.

I managed to focus my eyes long enough to look toward him. "It's her."

"Who, her?" Jackson asked.

I swallowed hard. I didn't want to say it. Not in a room with an Alpha and his cousin. Their wolves and their tempers were legendary. But there was no way around it. I had to tell them. I licked my lips. "I met my mate today, too. All the signs were there. Instant attraction, incredible smell. Visible shock and awe. Everything."

"But you and I only went to the..." Billy stopped talking and stared at me, his eyes wide. "You don't mean..." Billy's eyebrows lowered suddenly as he glared at me with surprising intensity.

I nodded. "It's Ruby, isn't it?" I glanced from one glowering wolf to the other.

"Ruby?" Jackson repeated.

I exhaled sharply then lifted my tone, making my words seem far more casual than they felt. "Yes, *Ruby*. My mate is a red-haired, gorgeous young witch who works at the florist in town. How about you guys?"

"No!" Billy practically yelled, slamming his beer down on the counter and causing it to fizz and froth over. "That's impossible."

I shifted my gaze to Jackson.

He was shaking his head. "You have to be mistaken," he said. "She's *my* mate. I met her earlier when I picked up Grandma's flowers. She's got long, red hair and..."

I huffed out an uncomfortable laugh and pinched the bridge of my nose. "Yeah, and blue eyes, pink lips, and an unmistakable silver aura of magic all around her."

Jackson looked at his cousin.

Billy slammed his fist into the frothy mess on the marble countertop. "Fuck!"

Yeah. You can say that again.

CHAPTER 4

RUBY

I ran home practically screaming after work. I'd met three men—*three*—all of whom I had an incredible attraction to. Were they all my men? Or was I supposed to choose between them? How did this work, exactly? It's not like magic was a precise science...

Could one of them be for Bella and one for Tiffany? Had I somehow called all three of them to me by accident? No, I didn't think so. There were no accidents or mistakes where Fate was concerned.

When I got home, I found a note Mom had left on the table.

Going to be late. Dinner's in the fridge. Love you.

I pulled out my cell phone and messaged Bella and Tiffany, barely able to contain my excitement.

Got AMAZING news! Come over as soon as you can.

Both responded immediately, saying they'd be over in about an hour.

Perfect. I put Mom's homemade chicken casserole in the oven and jumped in the shower. I smelled like a heady combination of roses and lilies. It was strange how much I loved the many fragrances of the shop but also found it extremely overwhelming at the same time.

Stepping out of the shower, I dried myself, and dressed in comfy sweatpants and my favorite hoodie. I was psyched for a night of hot chocolate and movies with my two best friends. That was, if they wanted to stay after what I told them! Hopefully they wouldn't feel jealous, since they hadn't found their Fated men yet.

I devoured the delicious and flavorful casserole Mom had made. She loved to cook from scratch, rather than choosing to use magic. She found it therapeutic and enjoyed the time in the kitchen. And I had to admit, her homecooked meals tasted better than the meals I could conjure up.

I was just putting my plate in the sink when the doorbell rang. "Come in!" I called out and a cacophony of sound burst through my front door. I couldn't stop the grin that spread across my face as I called out to them, "In the kitchen!"

Tiffany strode through the door holding bottles of soda.

Bella had blocks of chocolate in hand.

"So, what's the occasion?" Bella asked, straight off the bat, her eyes sparkling.

"I met him today!" I said with a squeal and a ridiculous little dance.

"Him?" Tiffany repeated, brow quirked

I nodded, an insane smile stretching my lips. "Well, *them* actually. But that's the next part of the story. You know... him. My man? The one we cast the spell for on All Hallows' Eve last year?"

Bella clapped her hands together and grinned at me. "Oh my God. That's awesome! So, it really worked? Who is it? Do we know them? It it one of the guys in town? Or—"

Tiffany put her hands up silenencing the conversation. "Hang on just one second. Did you seriously just say, *them*? As in plural, Ruby?"

She never misses a beat, this one. I bit my lip, unable to contain the nervous energy bubbling within me. I still hadn't worked out that part. "Yeah, well, I'm not quite sure exactly what's going on in that regard."

Bella leaned over the counter conspiratorially and rested her chin on her hand.

Tiffany sat on the kitchen stool beside her. "Tell us everything."

I laughed at the happiness fizzing through me and explained it all, from the moment Jackson had exploded into my life. How I'd felt and how he'd reacted. Then, what had happened when the other two guys had walked into the florish just an hour later.

"And they were all wolf shifters. You're sure?" Bella asked. She was standing to attention, her eyes wide and shocked.

We didn't have much to do with the shifters in the witching community to be honest. They didn't seem to like us for some reason. "Yeah, pretty sure. Well, two out of three of them were, anyway. Jackson, definitely. And the other big one. Both went all growly and basically couldn't speak when they met me."

Tiffany shivered and sighed. "Oh, that sounds so sexy."

I laughed. "Yeah, it kind of was. I've never experienced anything like it!"

"And the third guy?" Bella asked, hungry for more details.

I tilted my head to the side, thinking about what made him different. "Um... he was something else, I think. He definitely had some wolf in him, but he was smaller than the other two, and... you know what? If I didn't know better, I'd say he had some warlock about him."

"Really?" Bella asked, her eyebrows climbing higher up her forehead.

Combinations of witch and shifter blood were uncommon, which would mean that if I was correct, tracking down his lineage would probably be relatively easy. I thought about it for a minute. "Yeah. I'm pretty sure that's what it was, because he had no problems talking to me, even though I had the same reaction to all of them."

"More toward one than the others?" Tiffany asked, opening one of the chocolate wrappers with her long fingernails. When she got frustrated with the fiddly packaging, she flippantly waved her hand over the counter and magicked us up some platters of snacks and arranged everything to her liking.

I grinned. "Um, do you mean, if I had to choose?"

Tiffany shrugged. "I suppose so."

I pressed my lips together. How would I even start to evaluate something like that? They were all so unique, each with their own particular quirks and beauty.

"Well, I don't really know them yet, obviously, but Jackson— the first guy I met—he is just gorgeous with a capital G!" I grinned at them, heat flushing my cheeks at the mere thought of him.

"And the other two?" Tiff prompted.

"Billy didn't speak at all, but he was hot, too. He seems more of the bad boy type, which could mean trouble."

Tiffany laughed. "Sounds like my kind of guy. And how about the third one?"

"Hmm... he was the one that I think has some witch or warlock in him. He spotted me right away and had no issues chatting. He's smaller than the other two, but super sweet. The kind of persona you could easily be best friends with."

Bella put both hands out in front of her like she was stopping traffic. "Hang on a second. Are you saying you hit the trifecta? The boy next door, the bad boy, *and* the protective Alpha?"

I hadn't really thought about it like that and it made me giggle. "Well, when you put it that way..."

"Then how are you going to choose between them?" Bella asked again.

I shrugged and picked up a chip, munching on it. "Who says I have to?"

"Ruby!" Bella exclaimed; horror written all over her face.

"What?" I asked dramatically, rolling my eyes. "If they're all meant to be with me—and that was how it felt—why would I choose?"

"You may not get a choice in keeping them all. Wolf shifters don't share. When they mate, they mate for life. You know that." Bella said, shaking her head as if it were obvious.

I groaned. "How would you know? We pretty much have nothing to do with them."

Bella crossed her arms over her chest defensively. "I've heard about them, okay! They're very possessive, especially the Alphas. They'll never share you. Not well, anyway. None of you will be happy in a relationship like that."

I shrugged and continued to chomp on the salty chips and chocolate sweets before me. I didn't necessarily like the idea of dating all three of them at once, of course. Like, how would that even work? But at this point I was just enjoying the feeling of success. Our spell had worked! I looked at my friends and grimaced, a little crestfallen by their reactions. "Why are you being so negative about all this? I thought you would be happy for me."

Tiffany waved her hands as if raising a white flag of surrender. "I'm not. I think it's totally cool. If it's Fated, it'll all work out, I'm sure."

I looked pointedly at Bella.

She sighed and rolled her eyes. "Because it's totally unfair! That's why. How could you meet three guys in one day when we haven't met even one? And how are you going to handle three men, Ruby? Seriously. You've barely dated!"

She was right. I was still a virgin. In fact, all three of us were. None of the guys in the warlock community were keen to mess with us, and the humans had a natural aversion toward our powers as well, so they steered clear. "I know, but..."

"Do you think that maybe the other two might be for us, though?" Tiffany asked, grabbing a can of Coke and casually popping it open with a *crack* and a *hiss*.

"Ooh... maybe!" Bella said with a sudden grin on her face.

"Dibs on the bad boy!" Tiffany called.

"I want the boy next door," Bella said, staking her claim immediately after.

Then they burst out laughing like it was the biggest joke on the planet.

I dropped my head and stared at the white countertop beneath my hands, trying to get control of the anger that had started boiling up inside of me. I couldn't contain it. It wanted out. *Fuck, this was bad.* My fingers turned into claws and a sinister green smoke billowed from under my palms. My stomach was in knots, and the anger I felt was rooted deep in my soul and was unlike anything I'd ever felt before.

"Ruby... whoa... are you okay?" Bella asked, reaching out to touch my arm.

I groaned at her touch abut forced myself not to react. Not to slap her hand away as I wanted to. *Calm down.* I closed my eyes and forced myself to take deep steadying breaths. *Surely they were just joking. They wouldn't take my men. They're my best friends.* "They..." I cleared my throat, the tone of my voice strangely deep and uncharacteristically dark in its intensity. "They're mine. All three of them. They're mine."

I didn't know where the rage came from, nor the unfamiliar voice I heard coming from my own mouth. But the possessiveness I felt toward all three of them had me wanting to rip my friends' heads from their damn shoulders.

It didn't make sense. These girls were my best friends. I considered my sisters. These feelings were insane and marginally frightening.

"We were joking, Ruby. We promise. We're sorry." Bella's contrite voice penetrated the eseething red cloud inside my mind.

With no small effort I willed the feelings away. Finally, when I could speak normally again, I staggered toward the family room. "I have to sit down." I managed to make it to the couch, but magic still pulsed chaotically through my veins, heavy and strong, over-whelming me. I needed to use it, quickly, so I pulled it inside myself and turned it around to make positive choices. I whipped my hands through the air and all the food from the kitchen magi-cally appeared in front of me, spread out on my mom's large coffee table.

"Come join me!" I called out.

My friends sneaked into the family room, trepid and wary.

Bella was chewing on her lip.

Tiffany had crossed her arms over her chest in a defensive pose.

"I'm sorry," I said. "I don't know what came over me."

Tiffany slid onto one of the opposite sofas facing me.

Bella knelt on the floor and reached for some candy. "It looks like these bonds are going to be stronger than we ever imagined," Bella said, popping a red sweet into her mouth.

I nodded, feeling a little more sobered. "Yeah, I think so."

Tiffany laughed and shook her head, breaking the tension in the air. "We probably should have done a little more investigating before we dived into the deep end of such complex magic. But we didn't care at the time, did we? We all just agreed that it couldn't hurt..."

It had been a lot more than that, but we all liked to play down our abandonment issues.

I forced out a laugh, myself, retrospectively amazed at our foolishness. "And using Halloween magic probably increased the spell's strength and potency."

Bella giggled, enjoying her sugar. "Well, so what? You got three husbands for the price of one. I wonder what we're going to get?"

I couldn't help it, I cackled at that one. I felt better now the darkness had passed. "I guess only time will tell."

Tiffany relaxed and picked up the bowl of popcorn, placing it on her lap. "Do you really think all three of them are yours, Ruby? For real?"

I nodded, more certain than I'd ever felt in my life. "Yeah, I do." I knew it the way I knew I loved these girls in front of me. The way I knew I was a natural born witch. The way I knew my mother would die for me. Things that were all perfectly true and I knew instinctively. This was exactly the same feeling.

"So, when do you think you're going to see them again?" Bella asked, reaching for a drink to wash down her snacks.

I shrugged and settled back into my chair, letting the last of the tension in my body dissipate. "They'll find me. I told Darren that I'd be around tomorrow, being All Hallows' Eve, so we'll see what happens."

Tiffany grinned. "Leaving it up to Fate, huh?"

I matched her smile with my own grin. "Don't I always? It seems to have a mind of its own and there's no point in trying to fight it."

She rolled her eyes, then laughed. "Okay, so, what are we going to do for the rest of the night?"

The conversation changed to movies and work, our moms, and food—which I was grateful for—but that didn't mean that I could forget about everything we'd already discussed. The spell we'd worked last year on our birthday had called on the Universe. Magic. Fate. And it was pretty obvious that Fate had no intention of making any of this easy on us. Especially if my lovers were any indication of what Tiffany and Bella had in store for them.

But one truth remained and niggled at me as we enjoyed the rest of our evening... since when did three men get along well enough to share one woman?

Especially shifters...

CHAPTER 5
BILLY

I woke up on Halloween morning with a raging, nasty-ass hangover. Having found out my Fated mate was not only a witch, but a woman I'd have to share with my cousin and the part-warlock-wolf? I'd needed a stiff drink. And more than one.

Darren had gone home soon after dropping the truth bomb. He hadn't even finished his drink.

Then Jackson and I consumed every beer in his house and

moved on to my stash. It took a lot to get drunk as a wolf-shifter, and even more to be hung over from it. Our metabolisms were abnormally rapid and to even feel the effects of alcohol took more than most humans could consume before passing out cold.

"Oh... God..." I moaned from my place on Jackson's couch where I'd crashed for the night. I tried to get up but found no strength in my legs and instead, kind of rolled onto the floor. I groaned as the floorboards seemed to rise up to smack me in the face.

"Yeah, I know," Jackson said from somewhere in the kitchen. "You want hair of the dog or water, cous?"

I tried to lick my dry lips and found I had no moisture to even wet them. I was dehydrated as fuck. "Water," I managed to croak out.

Jackson walked over and placed a glass down on the small table next to me.

When I finally sat up, my stomach lurched at the movement and my head pounded with the rhythm of my own heartbeat. "Fuck." I ran my hand through my tangled hair, then brought the glass to my lips and sipped at the cool water. My queasy stomach threatened to revolt but I swallowed harder and pushed through the pain. I would *not* vomit.

Jackson collapsed into the armchair opposite me, his hand wrapped around a bottle of some sort of vitamin water. He looked as pale—and as shit—as I felt. "We hit the sauce a little hard last night, don't you think?" Jackson said.

I rolled my eyes. *Talk about a rhetorical question.* Pushing myself to my feet, I staggered back over to sit down on the couch I'd fallen asleep on last night. "Can you blame us?" I said, sipping on the water and wincing at the feeling of how fuzzy my tongue felt in my mouth. *Gross.*

Jackson laughed, laid his head back against the headrest, and closed his eyes. "No, I don't. And part of me still doesn't believe it."

I stared at him. "Which part? That you finally found your mate and she's a witch? Or that you have to share her ass with two other guys?"

Jackson put his drink between his legs so it wouldn't topple over and scrubbed both hands over his face. "Why do you have to put it like that, Billy?"

"Which part? *Oh.* The ass part." I was partial to a tight ass, so if we were allocating body parts... I took another sip of the water before putting down the glass. "I don't know if it was my imagination but... did she smell like a virgin to you?"

It seemed almost impossible. A virgin at her age. Especially when she was so fucking beautiful! But she'd smelled like innocence to me, which had made my damn wolf shifter practically dance with glee. It had been nearly impossible not to shift in that flower shop. I'd had to clamp down my jaw and fight with every cell of self-preservation in my body.

Jackson sighed and didn't even look up. "Yep."

I grinned, unable to help myself from teasing him a little further. "Then you'll only have to share her ass with us. Never anyone else. There's comfort in that, surely?"

That got him to look at me, his lips pulled tight and down. "Yeah, thanks for that. It's not reassuring at all."

I had to smile at that one.

Jackson was from an Alpha bloodline, one of the few in our pack. But we didn't give the Alphas any real importance anymore, nor extra responsibilities. We considered ourselves to be above that ancient hierarchical bullshit, and yet, Jackson still had the genetics of an Alpha. The size of one. The need to claim, protect, and dominate. The mere idea of sharing his mate sexually must be frustrating the shit out of him.

"Not a great time to be an Alpha, huh, cousin?" I qupped with a smirk.

Jackson got to his feet. "Just shut up, okay? I need breakfast. You want to come to Milly's?"

"Yeah, I think I need to." I forced myself to my feet and dragged my sorry ass out of the house and after him.

Milly's was one of the few retail establishments we had. Due to the fact the main town was a solid fifteen-minute drive away, we only had the essential four businesses—a gas station, a clothing shop, a doctor's office, and Milly's. Milly's was a café that served the best, greasiest burgers and heartiest breakfasts around. If the folks in town knew how good Milly's was, I was sure they'd come and eat out here rather than put up with whatever diners they frequented.

We walked the two blocks in complete silence. Once inside the diner, we found a booth and ordered the biggest, heaviest breakfast available.

"You guys sure are hungry this morning," Toni, one of the older ladies who waitressed there, commented. She ran her gaze over both of us and frowned. "You look like you could both use coffee, too."

I nodded. "Yeah. Thanks."

Toni picked up our menus and left to ring up our orders.

I sighed and glanced at Jackson. "So, what are we going to do about Ruby?" I tried to stop myself from shuddering with tingling pleasure at the sound of her name, but if Jackson's annoyed look was any indication, I hadn't achieved it.

Jackson sighed. "I don't know," he said honestly. "Obviously, we have to claim her, but then what? I don't want her living out here with us. The pack will have an absolute fit. And I doubt she'd want to, anyway. All the witches stay in town. They have their own community and we have ours."

My jaw dropped. *Was he serious?* "Are you saying you want to live in town?"

Jackson shook his head and huffed out a laugh. "God, no."

Hang on a second. Was missing something here? He surely wasn't actually suggesting that he wanted to live separately from her after we were mated? That couldn't be right. No wolf could do that. We'd never want her out of our sight.

"And you expect that she'll want to stay in town?" I repeated.

He nodded.

The reality of my cousin's stupidity hit me like a ton of bricks. If he thought that he was going to be able to just walk away from this woman, like he had every other woman he'd taken into his bed, he had another thing coming.

I rolled my eyes at him incredulously. "You really don't want her to be your mate, do you?"

Jackson looked down at the table and ran his finger over some invisible crack he could see and I couldn't.

I groaned and ignored the impulse to reach over the damn table and shake some sense into him. I needed to know what the real issue was, but communication wasn't my forte and it certainly was his. "What's your problem now, cousin?"

Jackson had always been a conundrum in our family, so strong, sure and capable, and yet he ran from responsibility at every turn, and had never shown the slightest interest in wanting to settle down—except when it came to building his house. That had come as a shock to everyone. He'd been the only one in our whole pack who wanted to build a big family home, just for himself. No mate. No children. And no plans to fill it any time soon if his screwing around over the past ten years was anything to go by.

"I don't have a problem," Jackson said, puffing up his chest at me.

Toni arrived with our food.

I sighed with relief, even though my stomach roiled at the sight of the bacon, fried eggs, and sausages. I knew I'd feel better once I'd consumed it all.

"Really?" I asked, picking up my knife and buttering a piece of golden toast. "You want to claim the virgin witch, who just happens to be your wolf's mate... but then you're going to leave her in town and just move on with your life out here? I don't think so." I certainly wasn't going to do that. If that woman was mine, she would be sleeping next to me every night, and I'd be sinking my cock into her as often as she'd allow. But that was just me.

Jackson dug into his plate of pancakes first, pouring maple syrup over the stack, before digging in like a man starved.

I glanced around the cafe, for the first time ever wishing the warlock-wolf would pop up. He had an uncanny ability to be in the right place at the exact moment he was needed. Not this time, though. *Damn.*

"Who are you looking for?" Jackson asked between mouthfuls.

I stabbed a sausage and put it to my lips, the greasy oil dripping off the end before I could take a bite. "Darren. I thought he may have a plan that might actually work."

Jackson growled at me, a deep, threatening noise.

It made the hairs on the back of my neck stand on end. And it horrified me to realize that every wolfy part of me wanted to submit to that sound. To kneel, expose my throat, and let the Alpha know that I was no threat. But I wasn't doing that. We weren't in animal form, and he wasn't my Alpha in this setting. He was my stubborn-ass cousin who needed to check himself.

So, I ignored my animal instincts and shrugged, looking down at my plate to distract myself from my inner wolf's feelings. It took a conscious and concerted effort to stand up against Jackson when he was in this sort of state. I cleared my throat. "I'll go find him after breakfast." Then I kept eating, quietly annoyed at the fact I could barely lift my head with the Alpha glaring down on me.

He shouldn't do that. He had no right to force me to submit to him. I wasn't doing anything wrong.

And the more I thought about it, the more annoyed I became. My hands curled into fists as my wolf barked in protest inside my mind. I clenched my teeth and lifted my gaze to glare at the Alpha sitting opposite me. And I was just about to tell him where he could shove it, when a hand landed unexpectedly on my shoulder.

"I was wondering where you guys were. Move over, Billy."

I'd never been more glad to hear Darren's happy voice. The tension eased out of me as I focused on his soothing presence. Hopefully Jackson would back off now. I nodded in response to Darren's request and moved over on the booth seat, pulling my plates of food with me along the table. Then, realizing I was being rude, I offered Darren a plate. "You want some?"

"Nah, I'm good. I already ate. What happened to you two last night? You look like death warmed up."

I glanced over at Jackson, who was still doing his Alpha trick, growling and glaring.

Darren didn't seem to feel it as he continued to smile and look relaxed. Another advantage to having mixed blood, I supposed.

I decided to answer his question, since Jackson seemed incapable. "We got drunk."

Darren stared at me and then at Jackson. "Seriously?"

"Yeah, why?" I asked, forking the fried eggs into my mouth. My stomach was mercifully beginning to settle, and the coffee was helping to ease my headache.

"Oh, nothing. I'm just surprised, I suppose. I thought you'd be celebrating at finding our mate, not drowning your sorrows."

I glanced across the table at Jackson.

He'd stopped glaring at us, and instead was now fiddling with the napkin in front of him, looking as uncomfortable as I felt.

Darren was right. We should have been celebrating, shouldn't we? Finding Ruby was a good thing. *The best thing.* "Yeah... well," I began, "both of us were a little shell shocked to say the least."

Darren turned to look directly at me. "At which part? The witch thing? Or the fact you have to share her?"

God, he's blunt! I just stared at him. Darren definitely had more balls than I'd ever given him credit for.

Jackson growled softly in warning.

Darren stared at the Alpha for a moment, then... laughed at him. He laughed!

I looked from Jackson to Darren, then back to Jackson. *What the hell?* How did Darren ignore the Alpha stare like that? Regardless of how he did it, I wanted to know his trick!

"Both, huh?" Darren said, taking Jackson's non-verbal response as confirmation. Then he turned and smiled at the waitress as she walked past. "Toni, could you grab me a cappuccino to go, please?"

"Sure, hon," she said with a smile and a wink that bordered on flirting.

Since when was Darren so popular?

Darren turned to us, placing both hands on the table, palms down. "Look. I know you guys don't want a witch as a mate, and you certainly don't want to share. And no offense, but I don't want to share, either." He stopped talking and shrugged. "The witch thing is an advantage as far as I'm concerned, so I suppose I've only got one thing to worry about and not two."

I swallowed hard. He was taking this way better than we had. "Yeah, I can see that. So, what are we going to do about it?"

Darren grinned at me. "What do you mean? What are *we* going to do? This is Fate's choice. There's no question here. There's no fight to the death or asking her to choose. It just is what it is."

Jackson stared at him like he'd lost his mind, and finally

managed to find his tongue. "What are you talking about, Darren?"

Darren turned to accept his takeaway cup from Toni and stood up, shaking his head at us like we were bloody simpletons. "You guys really don't understand the concept of Fated Mates, do you?"

I glanced at Jackson, who looked distinctly annoyed at being told he didn't know something that was at the core of wolf shifter society. I tried not to laugh as I turned back to the warlock-wolf. I was liking this guy more and more by the minute. "Explain it to us, then," I countered. "Since you're the expert."

Darren smiled. "We have all been, quite literally, designed for her. She won't be happy with just one of us, and we will never find happiness without her. If you guys think you have a choice about all this, you're dead wrong. So, I suggest you wrap your heads around it and fast, because I'm going to see her tonight."

"Where?" Jackson barked out, his wolf slipping, bristling at the challenge.

Darren's gaze slid over to the Alpha, then he grinned, white teeth flashing against his lips. "She's a witch, and it's Halloween. All Hallows' Eve. The most powerful night of the year for the witches. She'll be out in all her glory tonight and personally? I intend to find out just what she can do." With that, he walked off, leaving Jackson and I to wonder what the hell had just gone wrong.

CHAPTER 6

RUBY

My mom had made me an epic little black dress with her magic for Halloween. It was meant to be "modern witchy" with some gothic flare. It was cut low in the front and clung tightly to my waist and sported an incredible pentastar halter neckline. But personal doubts niggled at me, and I wasn't sure. The dress itself was stunning, but did my tummy look too big? I was a bit on the voluptuous side... Did my ass stick out too much at the back?

"Hey, Mom, do you really think this outfit is flattering on me? I'm not sure about the length. It's pretty short."

My mother laughed at me from her place on my bed. "You look incredible, honey. You are the embodiment of youthful perfection. And the LBD style was practically designed for women who have tiny little waists like yours! Plus, with the classic black witch's hat?" She made a kiss in the air. "Magnificent, darling."

Hmmm… if you say so. I turned once more and stared at my reflection in the mirror with disappointment. The image I had of myself in my head was never quite what I ended up seeing in the mirror. I sighed, not entirely satisfied, but not unhappy either. Mom had made this outfit with love. She knew what the modern fashions were, and she had really nailed it. I was just feeling more self-conscious than usual.

There was a pause, then Mom said, "Why do you ask? You don't usually care so much about what you wear—especially on Halloween when most of your friends will either be in full gruesome getup, or not dressed up at all. Is there someone special you're trying to impress tonight?"

My heart fluttered as I felt the pull of my mother's words, the undercurrent of an enchantment I couldn't fight. Since I was a child, it had been hard not to tell her the truth. The whole truth, and nothing but the truth. I just felt compelled to be honest with her. Whether or not she actually put a spell over her words, or whether it ran deeper, more ingrained than that—like a natural mother-daughter-bond—I wasn't sure. I'd never had the courage to ask, and I'd never had the strength or true need to fight against her. She always had my best interests at heart, after all.

"Yeah," I said, hedging my bets with something general. I didn't have to get too specific. "I met someone yesterday at work, and he said he might pop by tonight." I turned to the left, then the right, inspecting myself in the mirror one last time. *I looked okay,* I supposed as I pulled on the finishing touch—the matching witch's hat. But all I could see were my faults. The things I would remove if I had the choice.

Witches weren't supposed to use their magic to permanently alter their bodies. It was one of the few rules we had in the community. Transformational magic was meant to be for short-term use or only in a dire emergency. Not because you thought your nose was too big or you didn't like the way your ass looked.

My mother's head popped up and her eyes widened with sudden curiosity. "Oh, really? What's his name? Do I know him?"

I turned toward my mother, who was sitting on my bed like any friend of mine would. I wanted her advice on the odd situation I'd found myself in, but I was unsure how much I should reveal all at once. We hadn't told any of our mothers about the spell we'd cast last Halloween. And after my mother's failed attempt at one relationship—my father—she'd given up on romantic love entirely. She'd never even hooked up with anyone else again ever since. She was one and done.

What would she say about the fact I had three men vying for me? And even worse, how would she react to the fact thatI wasn't sure I even wanted to choose between them?

My stomach dropped and my chest tightened with anxiety at the mere thought of telling her. She'd think I was some sort of... loose woman, when the complete opposite was the truth. How could I make her understand the pull of Destiny and Fate? "His name's Darren, and I don't think you would have met him. He lives out of town."

My mother stood up from her spot on my bed and smiled. "Darren. Well, that's a nice name. I can't wait to meet him."

She was so beautiful, trying to play the "cool mom", best friend-type of role. And I loved her so much for it. I knew she wanted to ask a thousand other questions but was holding back, letting me divulge what I felt comfortable with in my own time.

I laughed. "Yeah, maybe not just yet, Mom. Maybe wait until

I've spent more than five minutes with him first?" And not before I worked out what I was going to do about the whole *three-men* thing, and the wolf shifter issue. A lot of witches and warlocks didn't like the wolf shifter packs. I'd never been sure why, beyond the fact that they were obviously different from us.

But I trusted the magic that had brought them to me and was fully prepared to find out everything about them that I needed to. We'd make this work—somehow.

Mom ignored my comment about not wanting her to meet Darren and changed the subject. "So, what are you party girls planning on doing tonight?"

You mean on our joint twenty-second birthday? Not much. I shrugged. "Not a lot. We said we'd dress up and walk around town. See what was going on. How about you, Mom? What are you doing tonight? Something with the Coven? Or just Rebecca and Kathy?"

Rebecca and Kathy were Bella and Tiffany's moms, and the three of them were almost as close as we were.

"We're going over to Kathy's later, thought we'd cast a little magic," my mother said, waggling her eyebrows as though it was naughty or taboo that they could throw a spell or two together.

Our mothers were all powerful witches and probably could have trained to become healers or teachers. But instead, they'd raised us, putting their time and energy into our well-being, while working menial jobs to pay the bills.

It made me sad and feel a little guilty sometimes that my mother had missed out on so many things. A good job. A husband. More kids. But hopefully, my mom's time would come where she'd feel truly free to be happy without worrying about me. Perhaps now that I'd met my soul mate—well, *mates*—I'd be able to move out and she could move on with her life. Maybe even start dating again? Start over!

I grinned at her and shared in her silliness. "Enjoy, Mom."

All Hallows' Eve was the most powerful night of the year for witches like us. If my mother or any of her friends wanted some special power for a spell, it would be available to them tonight.

Mom walked out of the room and headed down the stairs, clearly in a good mood.

I ran my hands through my hair, arranging the long red waves around my face before giving up on attempting to make myself look any better. Grabbing my bag, I checked its contents. Cell phone. Keys. Lip gloss. *All good to go.* I bounced down the stairs and stepped toward the front door. "See you later, Mom!"

"Have fun!" she called, but didn't come out to see me leave. Normal behavior for mothers of twenty-two-year-olds all over the world. Not so normal for mine.

I opened the door and hesitated, one leg lifted to take a step outside. Was she hiding something? Should I go investigate? My cell phone beeped in my bag, and I rolled my eyes. That would be Bella. I was late. I *had* to go now. No more dawdling. I went out the door and headed down the street. Tiffany lived one block away and Bella, two.

We often joked that our mothers should have bought one large house and raised us together in some sort of single mothers commune. But with all our strong personalities, it was probably a good idea to put a block or two between us.

I crossed the street and waved at our neighbors, who were heading out to trick-or-treat with their kids. *How sweet.*

"You look awesome, Agnes!" I called out to the little girl who lived directly across the street from us.

She had red hair too, something she loved having in common between us. But her hair was tied up in cute pigtails and she was dressed as a zombie, with fake bloody gashes over her face, and a weird, home-made white sheet costume. She grinned at me and waved back, her front teeth still missing, making her look like some sort of ridiculously adorable gummy shark.

I smiled to myself as I kept walking to Bella's house. We lived in a normal community of humans, but there was a witch family on every street. The Coven kept their dealings and meetings strictly secret, and if we needed to perform a ritual of or gather, there was an old church with extensive grounds as well as an abandoned school outside of town that we used.

I liked being part of a community within a larger community. I didn't want to be isolated like the wolf shifters. Setting up your own town and excluding everyone else seemed unnatural, somehow.

As I turned to stroll up the sidewalk to Bella's house, I giggled to myself as I drank in the delightful and entertaining sight before me. Bella had decorated the house as she always did. There were cobwebs and spiders, skeletons, as well as a large plastic witch out the front. Why she wanted to copy the humans that much when the effect was so comically tacky was beyond me. I mean, it was fun, but so cliché!

The door swung open before I could even knock.

"You didn't dress up," Bella said, her accusatory tone as obvious as her narrowed gaze.

"You know that if you used some of your magic to decorate the house, it would look a thousand times better." I motioned to the human decorative crap around her front yard and grinned in return.

Bella rolled her eyes and pulled me inside. "You *know* we can't do that."

I laughed at her purple wig and hat. "Are you seriously wearing that?"

"Yes. Why not? We said we'd dress up."

"Yeah, but..." I whispered a few words of magic and conjured up a broom to go with my black velvet witches' hat and complete my outfit. Now, my look mimicked every witch's outfit from every popular movie ever made about uour kind. "You could at least try and make it look good."

Bella huffed at me.

Tiffany walked into the room, her zombie-nurse outfit on display for another year running. It was super short, white, and splashed with special effects blood.

I grinned at her. "Didn't want to make another costume this year, Tiff?"

Tiffany shrugged. "Why would I? It's not like I'm out to impress anyone. Speaking of which... what's with the new dress, huh?" Tiffany pointed her painted fingernail at me.

I twirled around.. "Mom made it. What do you think?"

Tiffany nodded approvingly. "It's nice. Your mom has a good eye for fashion that suits you."

I laughed. "Well, I do look just like a younger version of her, so she's kind of cheating, don't you think?"

There was a knock at the door and Bella rushed off to deal with the trick-or-treaters.

Tiffany closed the distance between us, her arms outstretched. "Happy birthday, Ruby."

I hugged her tightly. "Happy birthday, Tiff."

We'd been messaging each other from the moment we'd woken up this morning, but now we could eat, chat, hug, and laugh. All the things I loved to do with my best friends.

When she pulled back, she had a thoughtful look on her face. Her eyebrows were tugged down, and her lips were twisted.

"What's going on?" I asked, a little perturbed.

Tiffany wasn't the sort to have significant, deep thoughts, generally. She was always pretty easy going. She bit her glossy pink lip. "Nothing, really. I just... I was thinking about your guy problem."

"Guy problem?" I repeated with a playful nudge and chuckle. "Which part? The number of them or the wolf thing?"

Tiffany grinned at me. "I sort of like the idea of you having three guys fighting over you."

I pushed her with a grin. "Shut up, okay. I've never even had *one* guy interested in me. This is going to be insane." My breath caught in my throat, and I exhaled quickly to expel the stress building up. I hadn't even thought about that part until this morning, really. What on earth was I going to *do* with three guys? How did that even... um, work? I blush stole over me, and I tucked a red wave behind my ear.

Bella came back to join our circle. "So, what did I miss?" she asked, still holding the massive bowl of candy her mom had bought for the kids in the neighborhood.

All my favorites. *Yum.* I reached out and snagged a wrapped mini-Snickers and twisted the end to open it up. "Tiff was just telling me she's worried about my guy problem but hasn't elaborated yet."

We turned back to Tiff as one.

She rolled her eyes. "Yeah, thanks Rubes. Way to put the pressure on," she said.

I shrugged. "Just tell me? It's okay."

"Well, I was talking to my mom about the wolf shifters who live outside town..." She hesitated dramatically.

My heart skipped a beat. "Yeah? And?" Not that I'd wanted her to seek out information on my behalf, but Tiff had always been terrible at keeping secrets.

"I didn't tell her about you, don't worry," she added quickly. "I just mentioned some of them had come into town and asked what she knew about them."

"What did she say?" I certainly hadn't had the guts to ask my mom anything like that. I wasn't quite ready to reveal that much about my situation just yet.

"She was a bit shocked, actually. That I'd noticed them, I mean. But then she said, well... that they don't like us."

I stared at her. "What do you mean?"

"I mean... they're pretty much anti-witch. She said that they have a hierarchy of people they think are acceptable. Obviously, in their opinion wolf shifters are the best, then they'll tolerate humans, but witches...? Nope."

I put both hands up to stop her from talking, annoyed to even hear such things. "Hang on a second. You're telling me they just don't like us. That there's no good reason behind it? No explanations? We're just the bottom of the food chain as far as they're concerned?"

Tiffany nodded and grimaced. "Sorry, but yep. That was the gist of it."

Anger tightened my gut. It didn't make sense. "Then why does Darren have warlock in him? I could sense it. Maybe not a parent, but definitely a grandparent. It's there."

Tiffany shrugged. "I don't know, hon. You're going to have to ask him yourself."

Yes, I will, I resolved.

Bella's mom, Rebecca, walked into the room, dressed in purple and orange and other god-awful colored spots. She was a mixed bag, that one. "Hello, girls! Happy birthday and Happy Halloween."

Tiff and I smiled and thanked Bella's mom. She was the oddest of the mom group but had always been lovely to us.

"I'm heading over to Kathy's house," she said. 'If you girls decide to go into town, can you leave the bowl of candy out front, Bella?"

Bella nodded. "Of course. Hey, Mom?"

"Yes, hon?"

"Do you know much about the wolf shifters who live outside town?"

I almost smacked her for asking the question right in front of me. What was she thinking? What if Rebecca figured it out before

I had a chance to tell my mom? But instead of hitting Bella, I plastered a smile on my face and concentrated on whatever her mom was about to tell us.

Rebecca picked up her woven hippy bag and turned to frown at us. "Why are you asking about them?" She twisted the strings of the bag around her fingers and pulled tight, as though anxious about the question, which was weird.

"Ruby met some of them the other day, when they came into town to see their grandmother or something. Do you know much about them?" Bella asked, keeping her tone relatively normal considering she, like all three of us, was terrible at keeping things from her mother.

Rebecca slid her bag up onto her shoulder and moved toward the door. "I don't know much about them, I'm sorry," she said, but there was something off about her tone. Then she laughed nervously and swallowed awkwardly.

I glanced toward Tiffany, brow furrowed. Had she noticed it, too?

Rebecca continued. "They don't like witches very much. We were always just told not to have anything to do with them."

I had to step forward and ask, my curiosity winning out over my sense of caution. "Do you mean we've fought with them in the past? Is there some kind of paranormal war going on we don't know about?"

Rebecca chuckled. "Oh, goodness no. There's no war. No fight. It's just that..." She sighed. "The elders of the wolf pack think we're beneath them, and the old High Warlock who died last year didn't like them either. But that's all in the past, now." She shrugged, kissed Bella on the forehead, and headed out the door a little too quickly for my liking.

As soon as she was gone, I turned toward my "sisters" bubbling with renewed agitation. "I don't think we got the whole story there, but this just got even more complicated."

CHAPTER 7

JACKSON

Going into town on Halloween was like walking into a nightmare and not being able to escape. Humans, witches, and warlocks all intermingled and dressed up in costumes. And unless I was close enough to smell them, I couldn't tell which was which.

Or which witch was a witch. "Fuck. I hate Halloween," I said to no one in particular.

Billy chuckled from the passenger seat of my truck.

Darren said from the back, "You and me both."

I frowned, surprised Darren felt the same way we did. "Huh? I thought you'd like all these... shenanigans?" I slowed my truck as we passed through the town looking for a parking spot. There were people everywhere. Children in elaborate costumes, shops decorated with ghastly black and orange displays. A skeleton here, and a hundred carved pumpkins there. *Yuck.*

Darren chuckled. "God, no. Why would I? There's nothing respectful here about the power of witches and magic. If anything? It's a mockery of our culture. I can't believe the witches in town condone it."

Ha. I hadn't thought of it like that.

"There's one," Billy said.

I swung into the spot outside a restaurant with a large fish painted on the window. We didn't eat much in town, but this place looked decent with its trendy tables and nice white table-cloths. I turned off the truck and tried to ignore the tension and stress radiating through my body. I didn't want to do this. Any of it. I didn't want to be walking around town at the height of Halloween, and I certainly didn't want to go in search of our little shared mate.

Darren reached over and squeezed my shoulder. "Hey. If you've changed your mind, it's all good. I can find my own way back at the end of the night."

And give him free rein to bond with my mate? *Not a chance in Hell.* My teeth clamped down and I shook my head, that stupid Alpha growl rolling in my throat. I couldn't control it and I didn't like it, but it came out, nonetheless.

Darren laughed.

Impudent pup.

"Yeah, thought so. Let's go." He jumped out of the truck and slammed the door behind him.

I glanced over at Billy, who was staring at the busy streets, a grimace on his face. "You sure you want to live with him for the rest of your life?" I asked, only partly joking.

Billy looked over at me as he unfastened his seat belt. "The better question is: you sure you want to live without her for the rest of your life?"

I frowned as Billy shrugged and got out of the truck.

I'd been joking about living with Darren. *Sort of.* Because the truth was, I wasn't sure I could share my house—my space—with anyone for the rest of my life. There was a reason I'd built a big house and never invited anyone to come live with me. I liked my own company. And yet suddenly I was being compelled to not only accept one mate, but another two guys on top of that?

And that wasn't going over well with the lone wolf part of me.

You're not a lone wolf, you have the genes of an Alpha. "Yeah, yeah, yeah." I stepped out of the truck, locked it, and pocketed the keys. "Which way?" I had no idea where we were headed, nor what we were actually going to do with the night besides hopefully locate our mate. But Darren probably had a plan, so for once, I was following him.

"Let's just have a wander and see what's on offer. I'm hungry," Darren said.

I shrugged. Sounded like as good a plan as any, and I followed the two other men down the street.

A variety of food trucks were parked along the road and colorful food stalls lined the pavement. Even the restaurants were open, no doubt hoping to score some extra business. The fear on some of the human's faces when they saw me made my stomach churn. They shouldn't be instinctively afraid of me. I'd never hurt any of them. *Never.*

I shook off the uncomfortable feeling of being silently judged and instead focused on the scents of the food and candy all around me. The tightness in my shoulders lifted and my tense muscles relaxed. I sighed. Yeah, that was better. *And you know it's not their fault they're afraid of us,* I reminded myself. *It stops them from wanting to mate with us.*

"Jackson!"

I glanced up when my name was called out, and spotted a familiar woman standing with Darren and Billy on the sidewalk. Warmth spread through my chest. "Grandma. What are you doing here?" I walked up and gave her a hug, her body small in my arms. *I missed her.* I really had to make more time to see her like I had yesterday. I owed her that much.

She chuckled in my ear. "I think that's my line, Jackson. I live in town and I happen to enjoy Halloween. What are *you* doing here, tonight?" She was standing next to a stall serving cold drinks and cotton candy.

"We... ah..." How was I even going to begin to explain what had happened in the past twenty-four hours?

"Come to see if the pretty red head from the florist is around?" Grandma asked with a knowing wink.

My gaze slid to Darren and Billy, and I sucked in a deep breath. "Yeah... we did."

Grandma's eyes widened as she glanced from me, to Billy, to Darren, then back to me again. "No! She's... all of your mates?" she asked, sounding shocked but also, not. "Goodness."

I frowned, amazed by her intuitive understanding. "How did you put that together so quickly?"

She shrugged. "It makes sense, in a way. And Fate is never wrong. The last generation of the pack has produced three to four times as many males as they have females. I told your grandfather years ago that the only solution was to breed outside the pack, or to partner off the females with multiple mates. He assumed, of course, that you would just partner up with women from neighboring packs, but they don't have an excess either. But in this case... it seems like you're doing both."

I couldn't believe she was being so calm about it. I'd noticed the lack of females but had always assumed my Fated Mate would turn up one day. A wolf shifter, of course. A single woman to myself. I'd never thought *this* would happen. "I—"

Darren butted in and claimed my grandmother's attention. "I'm not sure if you remember me, Mrs. Davis. I'm Darren."

Grandma took the hand Darren offered and shook it with a warm smile. "Of course, I do, young man. Please, call me Rose. Your grandmother was one of my best friends before she passed on."

Darren's mouth dropped open. "I... I didn't know that."

I didn't either but wasn't surprised. They were the only two non-wolf-shifter women in our whole pack of their generation. It would have made sense for them to bond and become friends. They would have found a sense of unity in their shared differences.

"Oh, yes. And she was a truly good-hearted woman. I can see you have inherited a lot of her." Grandma stared at Darren for a long moment then smiled. "You must be happy to find out that your Fated Mate is a witch as well?"

Darren grinned. "Well, yes. I am."

Grandma beamed, taking the news of our situation better than any of us. "Well, I can't wait to meet the girl. I came into town hoping she'd be working, but Andrea said she isn't rostered on until tomorrow."

"We're hoping to find her tonight, as well," Darren said. "She told me today that she'd be around."

"Well, I can't help you there, I'm sorry. I wouldn't even know whom to point you towards, or ask. The witches are pretty secretive in town. Most of the humans don't even know they exist."

I frowned. "How do they hide themselves so well?" Surely there would be too many unusual things about the witches for a human to ignore?

Grandma waited a moment, smiling as a group of teenagers

walked past, then continued. "Well, for one thing, they look as human as I do. And they have a church outside of town that I believe they use for Coven meetings."

"Could she be there tonight then?" Billy asked, jumping into the conversation.

Grandma shrugged. "Who knows? Your guess is as good as mine."

Darren shook his head. "No. She said she'd be around town. She made a point of mentioning it. I think she wants us to find her."

"Then go look for her!" Grandma said, fluttering her hands at us with a big smile on her face.

I bent forward and kissed my grandmother on the cheek. "Thank you."

She cupped my cheek in an affectionate gesture, her eyes twinkling, then headed off in the opposite direction.

We turned as a group and surged into the crowd once again.

"She's so lovely," Darren beamed as we made our way down the street between the stalls and the humans dressed as demons, witches, and ghosts. "I wish my grandmother was still around." He shook his head with a note of sadness.

I glanced at a guilty-looking Billy. We both knew we were lucky to have her in our family, and we didn't give her the respect or time she deserved. We'd definitely have to change that.

"I think I see her," Darren said, stopping dead in his tracks.

"Where?" I demanded, looking around and inhaling sharply. I couldn't smell her over the top of all the Halloween festive nonsense, and my senses were the most heightened of the three of us.

"There! In the little black dress... Look, just follow me." Darren took off through the crowd and across the street, homing in on our mate like a trained bloodhound.

Billy and I chased after him.

I found myself quietly annoyed that I wasn't the one taking the lead. A stupid thought, but even so... Then I saw her, andmy damn heart stopped. *Damn, she's beautiful.*

Darren walked right up to her.

She turned to smile at him and her whole face lit up. She stared at him the way I yearned for her to look at me. With happiness and shyness, and healthy dose of desire.

Then she said something, and Darren pointed toward us.

Ruby's gaze flicked straight toward me, and our gazes met with the nerve-jangling clash and raw heat of a new sword being forged.

My wolf howled inside of me, dying to bust out—to meet his mate in the flesh. My skin tingled and I locked my jaw down to stop myself from shifting on the spot. *The pack elders would have my head for revealing our kind.* I closed my eyes and froze where I stood, fighting to keep my ravenous and excited shifter under control. The last thing I needed was to wolf out in the middle of town, in front of my mate and every human around on Halloween. That would break several of our laws, not to mention probably terrify my mate.

I clamped down on my shifter hard, though he fought me every step of the way. But when I finally managed to shove him way down with the promise of a long run when we got home tonight, I opened my eyes again and found everyone staring at me. Heat flushed up my cheeks and I shoved my hands into my jean pockets as I walked forward to join the group. "Hey," I said, tilting my head up at Ruby in greeting.

"Hey, Jackson," she said back, her face as flushed as I expected mine to be.

She wore a spectacular short black dress that highlighted every curve of her body. Every twist and turn called to me, begging me to run my hands over them, and sink my teeth into...

"Guys, these are my friends, Tiffany and Bella," Ruby said, calling me back and away from my fantasies.

"Hey," I greeted them.

Billy just nodded. Was he having trouble speaking again as he fought down his own inner wolf? Probably.

Darren jumped in, the only one who had his head about him. "Hey. I'm Darren. This is Billy and Jackson. It's nice to meet you both."

The girls grinned at each other.

When I was finally able to drag my gaze away from Ruby, I looked over her friends. One of them was a gorgeous blonde whose outfit was a little too risqué for my tastes. The other—the brunette—was super cute too but dressed in the weirdest Halloween costume I'd ever seen.

My mate was by far the most attractive and most serene. But I wasn't biased. *Not at all.*

"So, do you guys come in for Halloween every year?" the blonde one—Tiffany, I thought—asked.

I shook my head, unable to answer properly. *God, this was embarrassing.*

Darren chuckled, saving the day yet again. "Nah. We're not the biggest Halloween fans to be honest. We just came in to see Ruby again." Darren stared at our mate.

She smiled at him then glanced up at me.

That was the moment I knew that she *knew*. That all three of us were hers, and she was ours. I stepped closer, my tongue loosening as my wolf retreated at my command. "The humans around here are a little freaked out by our presence here. Can we go somewhere a little less... crowded, maybe?"

Ruby glanced at her friends, "Well, um..."

Tiffany grinned and linked arms with the brunette, Bella. "No problem at all. We're gonna grab something to eat. We'll catch you later, Ruby."

Bella looked like she was about to protest, her eyebrows drawn low over her eyes in a frown. But when she opened her mouth to say something Tiffany hauled her away and we were left standing in the street with Ruby, shining brightly, her Fated wolf pack clustered protectively around her.

I stepped a little closer.

Ruby had to tilt her head back to look at me. She was a tiny thing.

I could tuck her up and carry her around with me if she wished it.

"Where do you want to go, Jackson?" she asked, then licked her lips, staring up at me with her huge, emerald green eyes.

I shrugged. "Anywhere's good, although someplace quiet would be best."

Ruby pressed her lips together then tilted her head as she offered a solution. "How about we walk for a bit and see where it takes us?"

A growl rolled through my throat at the suggestion. *Hell, yes!* But I swallowed hard, trying to force the sound down.

She didn't so much as flinch at my natural reaction. Instead, she just smiled as she started to walk away.

All three of us fell into step and began to follow her.

RUBY

My *Fated Mates!* Frenetic energy buzzed through me unlike anything I'd ever felt before. I wanted to squeal and scream; to jump up and down with excitement. But that would have appeared juvenile. And I didn't want the three gorgeous men who were following me—literally following me—to think I was a child. I was a young, but grown woman, regardless of fact I was still a virgin.

It was already plainly obvious that all three of them were

older than me, but by how much? And how much experience would they have? Because mine was practically non-existent.

We cleared the edges of the shops on Main Street and the crowds began to thin out and disperse.

My plan was to walk the three wolf shifters the long way back to my house, and if I wanted to invite them in for a drink or something, I could. If I didn't, if I wasn't comfortable inviting them into my mother's house for any reason, I could just keep walking and do the loop back to the shops. But I wasn't going to tell them that was the plan. For now, we were just walking. "Hey, how old are you guys?" I asked, tossing the question over my shoulder as I waited for them to catch up.

Darren jogged up to my side with a grin on his face. "You want the four-one-one on all of us?"

I laughed. "You can do that?"

He shrugged. "Sure. It'll save some time."

I nodded. "Okay, great. Go for it."

We stopped at the edge of a road.

Darren turned to the other two men, both of whom were frowning at him but not speaking.

Interesting...

Darren gestured at Jackson, the biggest of the three. "Jackson's twenty-eight, a jack of all trades, and an Alpha wolf. Did you pick up on that already?"

I nodded. "Yeah, it's a bit hard to miss."

He grinned. "Your instincts are in good shape then." Darren tilted his head toward the third of my Fated Mates. "And this is Billy. He's Jackson's cousin. He's twenty-seven and a plumber."

Out of sheer curiosity, I had to ask. "And a... beta wolf? Do you guys still use those terms?" I'd done a little reading today about wolf shifter packs, but the internet had little on what true paranormals were like, so I wasn't sure I could trust it as a good and true source of information.

Darren shrugged. "Kind of. We're not a traditional pack in that sense. We don't really have a hierarchy where one member is higher than another, unless there's an emergency or an attack. Then we would revert instinctively to the natural pack hierarchy. And yes, Billy would be there, fighting right beside Jackson."

I wanted so desperately to reach over and touch Darren. My fingers itched and ached, so I twisted them together in front of me as we walked to stop myself from doing exactly that. He was so warm and vibrant. But I didn't dare just yet. It felt too early. Not to mention I'd have no way of knowing how the other two would react to my initiating physical contact. I definitely didn't want to instigate a pack fight.

"And how about you?" I asked Darren.

"Me?" he said, his dark eyes twinkling with mischief. "Guess."

I bit my bottom lip. "But I might be wrong."

He shrugged again. "Doesn't matter."

Okay... "I think you're probably a tradesman too, though I'm not sure which kind. You're closer to my age, so maybe something like twenty-three? And as far as your wolf origins go, I know you have witch in your genetics, but it's more distant than parents. So maybe a grandmother or grandfather?"

Darren laughed and grabbed me about the waist, hugging me against his body and swinging me around so that my feet lifted off the ground.

I squealed in shock as much as delight, unable to hold the sound in, until he finally planted me firmly back on the ground.

"You're awesome," he said, with a big smile. "Yes, my grandmother was a witch, actually. I'm twenty-five and a sparky by trade."

I glanced at the other two men who were now growling softly in their throats. I didn't really like the sound—it made my skin crawl—but I was also pretty sure the sound wasn't directed at me. I stepped closer to Darren. "Why are they doing that?"

He grinned. "They're just jealous I touched you, but it's okay. They'll get used to it in time."

I took the opportunity to ask the glaringly obvious but rather embarrassing question. "So... it's all three of you, right?" I couldn't bring myself to spell it out. How vain would I sound to just come out and ask if all three of them wanted me?

He lifted one eyebrow. "All three of us *what*?"

"You know..." I said, gesturing between him and me, and the other two men and me.

He laughed again, the sound putting me at ease. "Are you asking me if all three of us are here for you? If we all want you?"

I nodded, trying to stay calm, though a heated brushfire stole up my cheeks.

"Of course, we do," Darren said. "All three of us believe you're our Fated Mate. Do you feel the connection with us too?"

I nodded, though the terminology was not entirely familiar to me. "Fated Mate?"

"Yeah. It pretty much means that Fate designed us for you, and you for us. We're a perfect balance of personalities and strengths."

"Ah, okay," I said. *Soul Mates*. Destined Lovers. Something like that, anyway. So, our spell had truly worked after all! Tiffany and Bella would be thrilled to know. "So, is this common in your pack? To have three men and one woman, I mean? Because I can tell you, now, for the witches, this is highly unusual."

My mother was going to flip out when she found out.

Jackson growled louder and shook his head.

I looked over at Darren and scrunched up my nose. "How come they can't talk to me, and you can?"

He chuckled. "I think it's the witch in me? I don't respond to my wolf shifter in the same way they do. And much to his annoyance, I don't respond to Jackson's Alpha dominance thing either." He shrugged as though his differences were no big deal, then continued. "But to answer your question, no, it's not common to have three men to one woman in our pack. I've never heard of it, actually. And the reason they can't talk is because they're fighting their shifters back. At least, I think. I'll ask them later when we get home."

I glanced over at the two huge men and saw the strain in their jaws, the inherent anger in their gazes. "Are they mad at me?" I asked quietly, my stomach dipping strangely at the idea of them being disappointed in me.

Jackson and Billy both shook their heads and Jackson managed to growl out a garbled, "No."

Darren took my hand in his.

A frisson of excitement danced along my skin.

"Let's keep walking," he said and pulled me across the street.

I held his hand tightly and directed the group up the street around the block, and down my street. As we walked closer to my house, *my mother's house*, nerves began to creep in. My gut tightened and the hairs on the back of my neck stood up.

"So, tell me more about you guys," I said, not sure what I needed to know, but wanting to hear Darren speak all the same.

"I think we'd like to hear about you, Ruby. Tell us about your family, work. College, anything? Personally, I want to know more about your magic, too," Darren said with a grin.

I took that to mean that the other two probably wouldn't want to know about my witch abilities. "Oh... sure, but can I ask you a question first?"

He nodded. "Of course."

"How come wolf shifters don't like witches?" I asked, desperate to know. "I mean, it's obvious from your grandparents' marriage that not all witches are shunned by your pack. But from everything I've heard today from my friends and their moms, you guys generally have an issue with us. Is that true?"

Darren glanced over at the other two walking behind us.

I stopped, making the other men stop also. I turned to look at the big men behind me and raised my eyebrows in query. "Well?"

When they didn't respond, I crossed my arms over my chest and stared at them.

"I want you to speak, too, not just Darren," I said. "It's not fair. How am I supposed to get to know you all if you can't talk to me?"

"Ruby, they can't..." Darren tried to excuse them.

But I was getting annoyed. If they'd come into town to see me, to court me or whatever the expression was, I wasn't going to get a good feel for them with those ridiculous wolfish glares on their faces all the time. I may as well just choose Darren and be done with it. Release poor Jackson and Billy to date someone they could talk to.

The mere thought made my heart ache. Letting them go? *God... I really didn't want to.* I put those feelings into my voice, my disappointment and frustration rolling through my tone. I flicked my gaze at Darren. "Well, they can go home then, can't they? We're away from the crowds, and I'm not touching you, so they have no reason to let their animal half take over and rob them of their ability to speak. It's not fair on any of us. So, if they're not going to talk to me, they might as well go home, and you can come with me."

I lifted my chin in challenge, hoping it would be enough to drag them out of their wolf-bound isolation.

Still, neither Billy nor Jackson said anything. They simply continued to glare at me.

I threw up my hands. *This is insane. This can't work!* "Fine. Keep ignoring me." I turned around. My house was about five fences down. I could see the bells hanging on the front porch, swaying in the slight breeze. Enough was enough. Clearly Fate was drunk on spiked pumpkin juice. "I'm going home."

A hand snaked out, grabbed my arm, and whirled me back toward the group.

"Oh..." I gasped as I slammed into Jackson's chest and his arms wrapped around me.

I should have been terrified by his strength, his intensity, the way he was looking at me like he wanted to literally devour me alive. But I wasn't. Far from it. I wanted him to do everything to me that his look said he craved.

"Don't go," he said, and his teeth extended past his lips now. They were pointed and his jaw had changed. It was more angular. Stronger.

I blinked up at him. "Then tell your wolf to back off." I cocked my head in thought. "Unless you want me to work a spell to put him to sleep? I'm sure I could." I lifted my hand and wiggled my fingers. I didn't call on my magic, nor conjure anything. I was just teasing and bluffing *mostly* but was interested in seeing his reaction.

The growl that Jackson released shivered through me. One of his hands swept down to grab my ass and haul me against his body even tighter, fitting me into the cradle of his hips.

I gasped, frozen in place.

The other hand moved up to the back of my head, gripping my skull so that I was staring into the stormy blue eyes of an Alpha wolf. The focus of his gaze shifted when my lips parted so that I could breathe, my heart pounding in my chest like a runaway train.

He dropped his head and pressed his lips to mine more gently than I'd anticipated.

I moaned in my throat as a wave of heat swept through me. I could feel the veiled strength and wanted so much more of him than this kiss. His passions ran deep, I could sense them. This was only the tip of the iceberg. I ran my hands up his huge arms, over his neck and into his thick hair so I could grip his head and pull him closer. *Damn, he's big.* How hot and muscly would he be under this sweater?

Jackson groaned and pressed open my lips with his, using his tongue to sweep inside my mouth.

I shivered with desire, my belly tightening with liquid heat.

The hand that cupped my head moved lower, grabbing my other ass cheek so that he was holding my whole lower body firmly in his grasp.

I gasped against his mouth, stifling the wanton moan that rose.

"Ruby!" I heard my name being called as though from very far away.

Jackson froze against me, like a statue. His startled groan was not one of pleasure, but of pain.

I ripped my lips away from his and frowned toward the direction from which my name had been called.

My mother and her friends stood on the other side of the street, the anger in their faces a blazing mass of fury.

Oh shit! I couldn't extract myself from Jackson's tight grip. He was frozen, like a popsicle.

My mother raced across the pavement and reached out for me.

I glared at her as she stood in front of me. "Mother! What did you do?"

"What the hell are you doing with a pack of wolves?" my mother demanded, her eyes glittering with the silver of living magic.

If I wasn't so angry at the sudden intrusion, I'd be terrified of what she was about to do to my mates. "Unfreeze him, Mom. *Now.* I can't get out of here." I was bent backwards and at a rather awkward angle.. My gaze darted to Darren and Billy, who were both also frozen in place. "Mom!"

"Okay, okay," she said, and snapped her fingers.

All three men jolted forward in a strange way as though falling, then caught themselves as they came out of their stupor.

I managed to get my feet under me so that I didn't fall on my ass but stumbled a few steps away.

My mother grabbed my arm and pulled me to her side in a defensive and protective manner.

The guys took a moment to regain their faculties, then came together with a growl, redirecting their ire at my mom.

"Back off," my mother warned, conjuring a ball of fire with one hand and brandishing it toward the wolves—a very real threat.

"Mom! Stop!" I said, pulling down her arm. "You can't use your magic out in the open like this."

My mother finally seemed to hear me and dropped her hand down, though her best friends stood on either side of her like a military guard.

She barked at my men, "Go home. Now!"

Jackson glared at her, the Alpha in him standing strong. "We're not going anywhere."

Uh oh. Mom won't like that.

My mother glanced at her two best friends and as one, they spoke a single word, flicked their right wrists in the air, and then my men were gone.

Gone! Just fucking vanished into thin air. I gaped at the space where six hundred pounds of wolf shifters was just moments before. I pulled my arm out of my mother's grasp and glared at her. "Where the hell did you just send them?"

CHAPTER 9
BILLY

One minute we were standing on the sidewalk in town, glaring at the cluster of three older witches who'd interrupted our moment with Ruby—the hairs on my arms and legs had been standing on end as my shifter howled to get out—then the next moment, light flashed before my eyes.

I staggered like a drunk, legs weak, heart pounding, sweat rolling down my back.

I grabbed for anything to stop myself from falling to the

ground. My hands found nothing to grasp, and I bit the dust. Hard. My vision cleared as my head whirled, and my fingers dug into the dirt beneath my hands.

We were back in our town. Or at least I was. I glanced around. *Where were the others?*

Jackson's groan sounded a few feet away.

I pushed myself to roll over onto my back, breathing heavily.

"What the hell happened?" Jackson asked, coughing up a lung, his anger already on edge.

Darren staggered over, the only one of us to remain still standing; no doubt a boon of being part warlock. He took a deep breath and moaned as he straightened his spine and stood up, blinking rapidly. "They, uh, sent us back."

I pushed myself up using what little core strength I had left. "Who sent us back? And where the hell are we?" I blinked, my vision slowly clearing. I recognized the dirt I lay in now, the fence and the trees. We were actually just outside the wolf shifter community gates—discarded like trash.

Darren's lips kicked up at the sides into an amused smile. "Ruby's mother and her friends. When we refused to leave—or Jackson said we wouldn't leave—they cast a spell together to send us back here. Pretty impressive, actually," Darren said, his tone indicating he was absolutely enraptured with the witches.

I tried to growl and glare at him, to share my displeasure, but it came out weak and half-hearted. It felt like she'd sapped every bit of strength from my body. "Why do I feel like such shit and you're standing there looking okay?" I asked. It certainly wasn't due to physical fitness or strength, obviously, because Jackson and I were three-fold stronger than Darren as full-blooded wolf shifters.

Darren shrugged, nonplussed. "I assume my own magic gave me some measure of resistance to theirs. Obviously not enough to stop them, but to handle the impact of their spell better. You guys probably haven't had a spell cast against you before."

"And you have?" Jackson asked from where he sat with his head in his hands, nearby.

Darren nodded. "Yeah, a few. My grandmother used to teach us to use our magic a little when we were kids. And she used her magic on us, even if it was just to make some new clothes or food. It wasn't anything nasty, just common, day-to-day stuff."

I stared at Jackson, then back to Darren. I hadn't realized witches used magic for everything. Simple stuff like clothes and food? *Was he serious?* Why hadn't I been told about that? It could have come in handy.

Jackson hauled himself to his feet.

I followed suit, forcing pure willpower into my muscles to make them hold my weight. It was painful, but not unbearably so.

"Well, what do we do now?" Jackson asked, dusting his hands off on his jeans.

"We need to go get your truck, for one thing," I said, annoyed that we'd have to drive back into town and get it. *Fuck it. It can wait until tomorrow.*

Jackson stared at me, one eyebrow raised. "I don't know about you, but I could really use a run to get my blood pumping again."

My mouth dropped open. I couldn't remember the last time we'd shifted into our wolf forms and run through the forest bordering our community. I grinned. "You know what? Me, too." My wolf had been flexing his strength inside my mind since we'd found our mate. "It might make it easier to control them around Ruby." I hated the fact I couldn't even talk to my Fated Mate because I was too busy clamping down on my jaw and keeping my shifter in check.

Jackson nodded in agreement. "You want to come, too?" he asked Darren.

I assumed he offered simply out of politeness, because everyone knew Darren didn't shift.

Darren grinned. "I'd love to."

My eyebrows flickered up with surprise. *I'll be damned.*

Without further discussion, we all started walking the mile back to our actual town.

I had assumed that Darren simply *couldn't* shift, but then again, he was three-quarters wolf... so why I'd even assumed that, I didn't know.

It took us ten minutes to walk back, but by the time we got to Jackson's house, I was absolutely buzzing with energy.

The sun had dropped below the horizon, darkness had settled and spread its star-spangled shroud across the land. It was still Halloween, which meant it would be the perfect time to scare some local kids.

We dropped all our clothes at Jackson's place and let the magic of our inner wolves rip through us. There was nothing like it.

When I let go of my humanity my skin burned like I was standing too close to an open fire. Then the fur began to sprout, and my bones began to bend and break, reforming to accommodate the canine form. It had been painful the first few times, but like all shifters, I'd soon learned to embrace the feeling. A growl rumbled through my chest as I changed into a large, black wolf. Not quite as big as Jackson's, who stood half a head taller than me, but still big enough.

Darren shifted too, though his transformation was slower, and his wolf form was smaller than ours.

We took off into the woods, running as hard and as fast as we could, howling through the trees and rejoicing in this strange new adventure we were on. *Together.* And for the first time since we'd met Ruby, I was glad I wasn't alone.

Ruby

I WAITED for my mother to reply to my question and when she didn't, I threw up my hands in frustration and stalked back across the street toward home. She wasn't allowed to use any magic—let alone transportational magic—out in the open. Anyone could have seen her! *And where the hell had she and her friends sent my men?*

I stormed inside the house, not bothering to shut the front door because I knew they'd be following in a minute, anyway. My veins buzzed with adrenaline and anger, while my heart banged against my ribs in rebellion as my hands shook. I couldn't sit down. Couldn't stay still. Not for the life of me. I grabbed a bottle of water from the fridge and drank half of it in a few gulps.

"Ruby! What were you doing with those men?" my mother demanded as she raged into the kitchen, her best friends both hot on her heels.

"I was kissing them!" I yelled back, flinging my arms around emphatically so that water from my bottle sloshed across the room, splattering the cabinets.

Bella's mom flicked her hand and the water splatters disappeared.

I rolled my eyes. She hated mess.

My mother's gaze narrowed at me. "You were kissing the big one. Why?"

I crossed my arms over my chest and glared stubbornly at her. She had no damn idea, and it was none of her business. "Because I wanted to. Because he kissed me!" *And because I'm their Fated Mate,* but I'm not sure I want to say that out aloud just yet—especially with tempers flaring so hot.

My mother paced around the kitchen and her friends fell back.

Kathy rested against the wall.

Rebecca leaned against one of the cupboards.

We all knew it was better to give my mother room when she was mad.

"How do you even know a group of wolf shifters?" she asked me, narrowing her gaze.

"I met them at the flower shop yesterday," I admitted.

"All three of them?" Her brows quirked in what I guessed was disbelief.

I nodded.

Mom gestured with her hands in a rolling motion. "Well, go on then! I know there's a story behind all this."

Of course, there was, but how much did I really want to tell her? I closed my eyes, weighing the pros and cons of exposing all of it now versus later. No matter what, my mother would find out everything eventually.

The tug of her magic pulled at me. She wanted to know the truth.

I was going to struggle to hold back or moit anything, let alone lie.

"Ruby..." My mother's tone held a dangerous warning edge.

I groaned, opening my eyes to face the music. "Fine. Here's the truth, Mom. Jackson, Darren, and Billy say they're all my Fated Mates. And I feel the same way... I think. So, yeah, there's that." I added, before I threw up my hands and shrugged.

Mom fell into one of the kitchen chairs. "Holy shit."

My eyebrows rose up. *Holy shit?* That was her response? That's all she had to say?

Bella and Tiffany's moms began slowly backing out of the kitchen as one.

"We'll call you later," Kathy said.

Rebecca flashed an uncertain smile.

Then they hightailed it out the front door.

Smart move.

My mother jumped to her feet and began flicking her wrists and waving her hands around, magic zipped around our kitchen like a chaotic, roiling storm.

I stood as still as possible. This happened on occasion, and although my mother's magic at the moment was simply for baking bread, making food, and changing the colors of the cabinets, it wasn't wise to get in the way. I could be painted purple or mixed in with the cookies if I wasn't careful. So, I waited to see what would come out of my mother's mouth at the end of it all. And what, exactly, she was so upset about. I knew that the three-guy thing was a lot to handle... but my mother was usually more composed than this.

Finally, the white sparks stopped flying and my mother halted, turning toward me, her green eyes blazing with light. "You're going to... *mate* with three men?" she asked, her expression aghast.

I sat down at the kitchen table and ran a finger up and down its white surface. She made it sound so sordid, when all I'd managed so far was one single kiss! "I... don't know. I've barely spent any time with them yet. I just..." I shrugged, momentarily lost for words. I didn't want to fight with my mom about my mates. Finding them was meant to be a good thing.

My mother collapsed onto the chair opposite me. "This is all my fault."

My mouth dropped open. Her fault? How did she figure that? I was the one who'd conjured a Halloween spell calling for my one true love to find me. *Perhaps having Bella and Tiffany work the spell with me tripled the strength and called three men instead?* I had no ideas, truthfully, but this definitely wasn't on my mother. "Your fault? What the hell are you talking about, Mom?"

My mother ran her hands through the long strands of her red

hair highlighted with streaks of natural gray. She wasn't talking and that was always a bad sign.

"Mom. What is it you're not telling me? Talk to me," I said. This didn't look like good news. Anxiety began to replace the frustration and bubbling anger within me. What was going on?

"Your..." She cleared her throat with a rough cough. "Your father wasn't a human. And he certainly wasn't a warlock."

My chest tightened and my breath stuck in my throat. "What do you mean? You always said he was a warlock passing through town. That you didn't know much about him. That it just kind of happened." I'd always hated the idea that my mother had procreated with and conceived of me with a complete stranger. It made me feel unwanted... lost, unplanned. Which I had been of course, but it was so much worse thinking that I'd been a pure mistake and one my mother had probably regretted.

"Well..." My mother inhaled deeply, stalling whatever terrible fate she was planning on revealing to me.

"Well, what?" I demanded. "You're freaking me out, Mom. We've always been honest with eachother when it's come down to it. So, please, just spit it out!"

"I did know him," she finally admitted. "We dated secretly for almost a year before I fell pregnant with you. Then he just disappeared."

"Disappeared? Like vanished?" This was new information. Since when had *shooting through* after she got pregnant, turned into *disappeared*?

"Yeah, well, at first, I assumed he'd just left me. Abandoned me when I needed him the most. But no one's seen him at all since the night., And well, there are some strange things that happen to wolf shifters when they mess with witches.... And you know my parents weren't the kindest of people." My mother sighed.

I put both hands out in front of me, halting her next words like a traffic warden. "Hang on just a second. What did you just say?"

Mom blinked at me, clearly overwhelmed with the weight of her truth. "Which part?"

"Did you just infer that my father was a wolf shifter?"

My mother nodded and swallowed hard, running her fingers through her hair in anxiety. "Yes, Ruby. Yes, I did."

Suddenly everything in my world made sense—especially the fact that I had three wolf shifter Fated Mates. But how were they going to feel about my mixed bloodline? And the secrets I carried too...?

CHAPTER 10
RUBY

I jumped to my feet, my magic whirling through my veins, making it hard to sit down for even a moment longer. I wanted to fly to my three men. I wanted to blow the roof off the house. And strangely, I wanted a pizza. *Yes. Definitely a pizza.* But instead, I stayed put in my mother's kitchen and simply paced around the room. "How could you not have told me this sooner?" I asked. "I feel like I've been living a lie, Mom."

"I didn't know how to."

I grimaced at her and sighed. "You mean you didn't *want* to."

My mother slumped in her chair, defeated and crestfallen. "No, you're right. I didn't want to, Ruby. I didn't want this information to influence you in any way. I didn't want you to worry about your magic developing or where you fit in society. Or if you were going to, you know..." She gestured helplessly around us.

I groaned. "Going to what?" I asked.

She bit her lip, her brows raised plaintively. "You know... *shift.*"

I stopped pacing then and stared at her. Shocked.

No wonder I felt like I didn't have a place in the witch community! All of this explained everything. Like why I was powerful *enough*, but had always ached to run, to be free, and not be rooted to this community that everyone else felt was integral to their survival. But to shift into an animal? *Crap balls.* "Is that even possible? I mean, how would we know?"

"Oh, it's not going to happen now," Mom said with a shake of her head and a relieved smile. "Now that you've reached full maturity, you've gone past the time when it would have been. I was told that we would realize a lot earlier if your wolf genes were going to be dominant, which, considering how powerful your magic is, would be unusual."

I didn't want to sit down, but I didn't know what to do with all the excess energy bursting away inside my body. My hands were shaking from the stress of this life-altering revelation. "Okay. So, you're telling me I'm half wolf shifter? Which is probably why the men I'm meant to be with turned out to be wolves?" That part at least made more sense, which truth be told, was a relief.

"I'll give you that. But three?" my mother said, looking skeptical as her gaze darted back to me.

I shrugged. "That wasn't my choice. It's just... how it is. It's Fate. I can feel it, and so can they. I couldn't stand to be without them now, Mom. We're connected."

My mother sighed, glancing down at the table, seemingly trying to gather her thoughts. "So, what are we going to do now?"

I crossed my arms over my chest and stared down at her. "Well, for starters, you can tell me where you sent them. And I can go sort all of this mess out."

She nodded and sighed in a resigned way. "I'll drive you out there if you like?"

"You don't want to just zap me to the same spot?" I asked.

She stood up and shook her head. "They could be anywhere by now. I'll drive you to the outskirts of their township, and you can decide what to do from there."

I stared at her. "You're going to just drop me off? No more fighting? No arguing with Fate?"

My mother shuddered, as though letting me go off into the big world at age twenty-two was an ordeal she'd never thought she would have to endure. Then she nodded. "Yes. I'll behave. I owe you that much as least. Let's go."

～

Jackson

After a decent run, Darren decided to return home.

But Billy and I weren't ready to stop. So, we ran through the woods and instinctively moved toward the human town, the complete opposite direction of what I had planned. And in direct opposition to Council recommendations.

The closer we ran to the human town, the more likely we were to be spotted or hunted. So the Council had rules in place to prevent us from being hurt. They told us the story of a group of cousins, of three men who'd gone missing over twenty years ago, when we were young. Most of the pack assumed they were dead. Shot most likely and perhaps mounted on someone's wall.

But I didn't care what the humans had done in the past or would do to me now. I was in my wolf form, and I could feel the unbridled strength of the mating bond we shared with Ruby. It was like something fundamental had changed deep within me. I was no longer adrift. A lone wolf. A man who could be happy just spending the rest of his days alone.

There was something tying me to the earth now—calling me home. And home was now Ruby. I jumped over a log with ease, dashed around a tree like it was nothing, and focused on my inner wolf. I felt a tickle on the back of my spine, feeling the crescent moon's power in the sky, the dirt beneath my paws, and the scent of pine and earth and magic in the air. Wait. *Magic?*

I slowed down, tilting my head toward the strange feeling. I peered through the woods and its dappled shadows, deeper into the trees and past the town. Was that where the church was? The Coven's hallowed grounds? I longed to run that way, to explore and spy on what they must be up to on Halloween night. But I didn't have time for that tonight.

There was something else calling me now. An itch like a bolt of lightning on the back of my neck made me stop, turn, and howl instinctively to the moon.

Billy stepped up and howled alongside me. He felt it too.

Our mate was on her way. She was traveling, and she was heading toward our town. We ran, our paws churning up the dirt in the dark. We galloped along the border of the town, and I could smell her, distantly. She was coming. We finally made it back to my house. We jumped the fence and shifted back into human form.

My black fur disappeared, and I was able to see color once again with my human eyes. I panted from the run; my skin slicked with sweat.

Billy transfored next to me, his eyes shifting back to their normal color. He looked straight at me. "You sense her, too?"

I nodded. "I do."

We rushed inside and pulled on our clothes.

I should have had a shower, but I didn't want to waste a single moment in case I missed out on seeing her. "Where do you think she is?" I asked aloud.

Billy shrugged as he tugged on his shirt. "No idea. Would she even know where to come? Who to ask for?"

"Not sure. But considering it was her mother's magic that sent us back here, maybe she can follow it?" I couldn't stop myself from grinning at the thought of her being so near to us again. We didn't know anything about witches or magic. The crap we'd been told came directly from our Council and our parents, who encouraged us to keep everything pure. Untainted. Which was so hypocritical it wasn't even funny.

Plus, Fate had different plans for us. I pulled on my boots and grabbed my phone. "Let's go."

We went to the front door.

A tremor of unease worked through my belly. What was my father going to say when he learned that my mate was not only a witch, but that I would have to share her with two other men? I shuddered at the thought. My father had always hated the fact he wasn't a full wolf shifter. He'd worked hard to make up for his lack of strength and speed by breeding with my mother, a daughter born to an Alpha wolf. It had meant that my brothers and I were strong in ways my father never was. He'd hate that I was diluting our bloodlines once again, even if it was because of the call of my Fated Mate.

We headed into town.

I lifted my nose in the air, searching for the scent of the red-haired witch who I knew would soon capture my heart forever. But what sort of future was there for us?

CHAPTER II

DARREN

After I returned from my short run, I went to my parents' house. I wanted to tell them what we'd discovered and who we'd met.

"How was your night?" Mom asked, putting on the kettle to make a hot tea for my father before they went to bed.

I sat down on the couch, grinning at my father while Mom did what she needed to do in the background.

"It was amazing. I found my Fated Mate. She lives in town."

Shocked silence.

My father's gaze lifted to stare behind me.

I turned around to see my mother's mouth had dropped open. "The elders have prepared us for this," she said. "With so few females born in the past twenty years... your mate could be a human. Or a wolf shifter from another pack."

My father smiled at me, though it didn't reach his eyes and I knew he was disappointed that my mate wasn't also a wolf shifter. "So, she's human?" Dad asked. "What's her name?"

I inhaled sharply, surprised at how much I didn't want to disappoint my parents. My mother would hopefully be accepting of Ruby's heritage, but my father... I wasn't so sure. I forced a smile and spilled the beans. "Her name's Ruby. She's a witch."

My mother walked forward and sat down on the couch next to Dad. "A witch?"

I nodded. "Yes. I think it's great. Our children will be so much more powerful than me."

Mom looked down at her hands. "Well, this is a surprise."

"Why?" I asked. "You're half-witch, yourself, Mom."

"But I never developed my powers..." she began.

Dad slid his hand across her leg, taking her hand in his in a show of comfort and unity. "So, you felt the Fated Mate pull?" Dad asked, which was the only reason he'd married my mother. He hadn't wanted to marry a half-witch, but Fate had other plans for him. And if nothing else, he understood the importance of trusting Fate.

I nodded. "All of it. But... ah, I'm not the only one." It was my turn to glance away. This part was going to be even more difficult to explain to my parents. It would mean that they would know more about my sex life than I'd ever wanted them to know. I sighed. There was no avoiding it.

"What do you mean?" my dad asked.

"Well, you know how there's like... no females in our pack to mate with?" I said, leading them toward the conclusion.

"Yes?" Mom said.

"You don't mean..." Dad said, his bushy eyebrows drawing together to frown at me.

"I do." I nodded and took a deep breath. "Jackson and Billy are her Fated Mates as well. So, I suppose... if she accepts us all, we'll be a big family."

My mother's mouth dropped open again. "Ah... I've never heard of such a thing."

"You're going to share a mate with Jackson?" my dad asked, raising an eyebrow.

I knew what he was asking. How was an Alpha going to share with me? It went against their very nature. It stood in the face of his very bloodline. "Well... uh..."

Mom smiled at me. "I think Ruby will want someone like you, sweetheart. Part warlock and all heart. She's lucky to have you."

I stared at my mom for a moment, then grinned, a weight lifting from my shoulders. "Thanks, Mom. I think you're really going to like her." A sudden prickle of unease washed over me, and I frowned as a premonition flowed over me. She was coming. She was almost here. I got to my feet fast. "I've got to go. I think she's on her way here."

"Here?" my father demanded, his brow lowering as he jumped up from the couch.

My mother grabbed his arm. "Calm down, sweetheart." She looked at me. "Go ahead, sweetheart. We'll catch up with you later."

I smiled my thanks at my mother and raced out the door. Where would Ruby be coming from? Would she be in a car? Or would she be traveling on foot? Would she magic herself the same way her mother had forced us back here? I had so many questions and no answers.

I started walking along our road, around the block, and down the main street. If I were her, I would head for the few shops in town since they would still be open. I sniffed the air, the faint scent of Ruby's distinct smell on the breeze. I kept walking toward the edge of town. There were no sounds to betray the approach of any vehicle. No engines, no lights heading toward us. Then I saw her, and my heart began to pound.

She was still wearing that gorgeous little black dress with the pentsstar detailing, and her long red hair flowed down over her shoulders as she walked down the street toward me.

Adrenaline coursed through my veins, and I jogged toward her. I got within touching distance of my beautiful mate and couldn't stop the smile that stretched shamelessly across my face. "Hey."

Ruby smiled back, her green eyes lighting up even in the darkness. "Hey, yourself."

"So, you found us." I grinned, reaching over to grab her hand. "Do you want to walk into town?"

She nodded and pressed her body close to mine as we strolled back toward the light. "I'm so sorry my mom sent you guys back here," she burst out, as though she'd been holding it in and desperately wanted to apologize.

I chuckled. "It wasn't a big deal for me. I've traveled by magic before, when I was younger at least. But Billy and Jackson were pretty sick afterwards." I tried not to grin too much. Part of me enjoyed seeing the two powerful wolf shifters wiped out by something as small and innocent as a transportation spell.

"Yeah, I can imagine." She sighed heavily. "Mom and her friends really shouldn't have done that. They were all cast first, ask questions later."

"Why did they, anyway?" I asked. "Was it because we're a pack of wolves? Or was it more that your mom didn't like seeing her daughter kissing strange men on the street?" I chuckled at my own joke but found Ruby freezing up.

"Hey, I was kidding," I said, squeezing her hand in an attempt to try and soothe her nerves.

She laughed nervously. "Well, she's never seen me kiss anyone, I don't think. I don't date much. And yeah, she was pretty freaked out by you guys being wolves and all."

Don't date much. I was pretty sure that was an understatement judging by the unmistakable innocent scent surrounding my mate.

"Does she have a history with wolves? Or is she like half the paranormal population and just doesn't like others who are different?" I asked, then realized how judgmental I sounded. I quickly backtracked, "I didn't mean for that to sound harsh. My own parents are firmly against any outside breeding." *Despite the fact my mother is half-witch. The hypocrisy...*

"Even though you're part warlock?" she asked.

I grinned down at my mate. "Yes. Even though my mother is half-witch, my father seems to think we need to breed it out of our line."

We were almost at the first streetlight in town, so I could see the emotions flickering across my mate's face.

She was chewing on her lip and looking anxiously at the ground, then up at me. "Is that how you feel, Darren? That me being a witch is a negative thing?"

I stopped, feeling the time dwindling away that I would have her to myself. The other two would be here soon, and I wouldn't be able to do this with her. I unlinked our fingers and slid my hands around her waist, pulling her close so that our pelvises were connected. "Not at all," I said, answering her question while attempting to squash the need to shiver at the deliciousness of the contact. "I love that you're a witch. Any children we have in future will be powerful and thanks to you, extremely beautiful, too."

Ruby glanced down, straight at my shirt where her hands now lay, near to my heart. Her beautiful pale skin pinked up at the compliment or at the idea of children. I wasn't sure which.

"May I kiss you, Ruby?" I asked, feeling the prickle of premonition on my neck. Jackson and Billy were closer now.

She nodded, her lips turning up in a genuine, if not slightly shy smile.

I leaned down and pressed my mouth to hers. She was as sweet and sensual as I had hoped. I breathed her in, tasting only the tiniest amount of her lips. I tried to keep it gentle but when her tongue flicked out to lick my lips, a groan rose up from my throat and my hands tightened on her waist.

I slid my hands down to her firm ass and pulled her into the cradle of my hips. I used my lips to press deeper and met her seeking tongue with my own.

She moaned.

Every part of me rejoiced as I recognized my one true mate. In my arms. For the very first time. It was everything I'd ever dreamed it could be, and more.

Her hands slid up my chest to my neck, then moved through my hair, holding me to her as she pressed her breasts against me.

A surge of lust plowed through me. I wanted to snap my fingers and have her naked in my bed, beneath me. But my magic wasn't that strong and as I inhaled sharply, I could sense that the other two men had arrived. I heard a loud gasp and then the ripping of clothes.

Scratch that. *The wolves had arrived.*

I broke our kiss but held her tight.

She swayed, her eyes closed, and a moan still trembled on her lips.

I pulled her to my side and turned toward the road where two large black wolves stalked toward us. They must have just shifted because a pair of jeans was still attached to Jackson's leg. My heart pounded with exhilaration and a touch of fear. I whispered into my mate's ear. "When you open your eyes, don't be afraid. Jackson and Billy are in their shifter forms." I held her tighter.

Ruby yelped as her eyes flew open. She stared at the men, who prowled forward as wolves. She slammed her hand over her mouth, a frightened squeal emerging, though she tried valiantly to stifle it.

"It's okay," I said. "They are in complete control of their wolves. Don't be afraid."

Ruby nodded, though her eyes were as big as the now full moon above our heads.

Jackson moved closer.

I waved at him. "Hey, Jackson." I knew him by his pure size. Despite the fact that our pack tried to be modern and not judge a person by rank, the shifter genes still determined our size, our strength, as well as our leadership skills.

Jackson was an Alpha through and through, with his massive body, his ability to handle any situation, and his stare that could turn even the most pureblood wolf submissive. He stopped moving and began to shift back to human.

I squeezed Ruby's waist. "He's shifting back. Watch."

Before our eyes, the black fur melted away. The four short canine legs became two long human legs, and two muscled arms; and the man began to grow into his own huge form. When he was done, Jackson stood before us in full light, naked as the day he was born.

I struggled not to stare, and almost laughed.

Ruby's hands moved up to cover her eyes. "Oh my God," she breathed.

"Hey, Billy," I called out to the second wolf as he also transformed back to human form.

They were both huge and muscular and had obviously forgotten that humans and witches alike weren't as comfortable with nudity as wolves were.

"Shall we take Ruby back to your place, Jackson?" I called out. "Maybe grab you guys some new clothes?"

Ruby peeked through her fingers, then as she dropped her hands, her gaze found the ground.

"You okay with that, Ruby, or would you prefer to come back to my place where my parents can chaperone?" I asked.

She inhaled sharply and lifted her head.

I could only imagine what she was thinking.

"No. It's okay. Let's go back to Jackson's house."

Jackson nodded and turned away to march up the street toward his house.

Billy followed.

I took Ruby's hand to lead the way. "This way, beautiful."

CHAPTER 12

RUBY

Oh. My. Fucking. God. They were naked. Naked as a babe... naked! I clung to Darren's hand and stumbled into town after the two men walking in front of us.

They bent over to scoop up some clothes on the street, which I had to assume were theirs.

Had they shifted when they'd seen Darren kissing me? Probably, silly jealous things that they were. "Aren't they cold?" I whispered to Darren, unable to take my eyes off the flexes of Billy and Jackson's muscles.

They were absolutely magnificent to look at. So much bigger, stronger, and more defined than any human man I'd seen in real life. And most probably the reason my mom fell for a shifter. The thought made me frown. *What happened to my father?*

Darren chuckled beside me. "No. They're not cold. Shifters run a few degrees hotter than humans, so the temperature doesn't bother them. And as far as the nudity thing goes... sorry about that. Shifters aren't worried about exposing their bodies at any time of the day. It's just not a thing to be embarrassed by. With us shifting in and out of our wolf forms so often, a person's body just doesn't have the same... taboo."

I nodded. "That makes sense." So, I had to get used to a world where this was normal? *Whoa. Bella and Tiffany are going to freak!* "Why aren't you in shifter form, Darren?" I asked, my gaze dragged back to Jackson's body. His ass was perfection— round, sculpted, and strong. And his back. Jeez, could the guy be any bigger? He had huge shoulders, massive arms, and a perfectly muscular back. There wasn't an inch of fat on him, and I began to worry about what they were going to think about my body.

I wasn't big by any stretch of the imagination but compared to these two? I was a frumpy sack of potatoes.

"Me?" Darren repeated. "Well, I shifted this evening and went for a run with Jackson and Billy, but I came back early. I don't shift a lot to be honest. I'm not that comfortable in wolf form, personally."

I got the feeling that for Billy, he was more comfortable in wolf form than human form. "So, you don't like to shift then?" I asked, just to make sure I understood what he meant.

He pressed his lips together as though thinking about my question before answering. "I'm three quarters wolf shifter so I can, obviously. But I'm much more comfortable in human form, and if I could, I'd perform a hell of a lot more magic than I do."

"Oh?" I asked, excitement racing through me. "Can you perform many spells?"

He sighed. "Unfortunately, no. My grandmother has been gone for a long time now, and my mother refuses to practice any magic. So, maybe you or someone from your Coven could give me some pointers?" He sounded so hopeful.

I laughed. "I'm sure we could." I wasn't sure just how much magic a one-quarter warlock with little training would be able to perform, but why not try? It could be fun.

We continued to walk through town, or what little of a town there was.

"Are these all the shops?" I asked, glancing up and down the road.

"Yep. Pretty much. A café." He pointed at a small eatery. "Clothes and gas station. We go into town for all the big things."

If that was the case, then why hadn't I seen them more often? Did they shop during the night or something? "So, um, what's going to happen when we get back to Jackson's place?" I asked, chewing on my lip.

Darren glanced at me and squeezed my hand. "Those two can get some clothes on and we can chat some more, if you'd like?"

I nodded, swallowing the lump in my throat. My heart was hammering in my chest and if I hadn't been holding onto Darren's hand like a proverbial lifeline and pressing myself into his warmth, I would have been shaking all over. I'd never been so nervous in my life!

"Why? What would you like to happen?" Darren asked as we turned left off the main street and headed down a road with new houses.

I shrugged. "I don't know." But I did. Of course, I wanted them to kiss me. I wanted my senses to be overwhelmed. I wanted to find out if this was the mating, the relationship, and the love I'd prayed for, and called upon in the spell we'd cast last year on Halloween.

Jackson turned down a sidewalk.

Billy followed.

They headed up to the front door and disappeared into the house.

"Wow. Is that really Jackson's house?" I asked, staring up at the modern two-story abode that looked like it could hold a family of ten.

"Yes."

We stopped in front of it.

I stared up at the second floor. It was beautiful, with pretty shutters, big windows, and a welcoming, blue front door. "Does he live here alone?"

"He does," Darren said and then added with a grin, "for the moment."

I lifted an eyebrow at him. Was he saying that all four of us would live here one day? I certainly wouldn't mind. What an amazing house! And only fifteen minutes from my mom and town. Ideal, really.

"Come on," Darren said, and tugged my hand.

I followed him along the sidewalk, up the two steps and into the house. The inside of Jackson's place was as impressive as the outside, though it was kind of soulless. There were crisp white walls and flawless wooden floors.

Darren flicked on the lights.

As we walked farther into the house I was greeted with a fantastic modern kitchen, but it was devoid of color, warmth, or... feeling. Although, what should I have expected from a bachelor? My mother would have turned this place into a mess of purple and family pictures in mere minutes.

And if I were honest, my fingers itched to do the same. To

splash the walls with red, to add appliances to the countertops, and pictures to the walls. Maybe some fresh flowers in vases artfully arranged around the place. I dug my nails into my palms and reminded myself to calm down. This wasn't my house, and even if it was… I wasn't sure my magic would be welcome here.

"Hey."

The deep voice behind me made me jump. I twisted around with a smile on my face.

Jackson stood by the kitchen counter, now dressed in jeans and a black shirt, and wore a sheepish smile on his face.

"Hey," I said, twisting my fingers together in front of me, nervous as all get out.

He took a breath and pressed forward. "I'm sorry you saw us like that. We *were* dressed but then we saw you and we both shifted again. It wasn't intentional, and I didn't consider that you may be scared of seeing us in wolf form."

Oh, he was sorry about the shifter thing, not about the fact that I got to see them completely naked within two days of meeting them. "Oh, it's fine," I said, trying to brush off the fact that he'd caught me out. I'd definitely been scared. "It's something I have to get used to, right?" At least he was managing to talk to me now. That was definitely a plus.

Jackson nodded, agreeing with my question. His eyes darkened as he stared at me.

Billy stepped into the great room, his gaze going straight to me.

"Hi," I said, feeling strangely awkward and excited at the same time.

Billy nodded back, but once again was completely mute.

I wasn't sure I'd even heard his voice yet.

"Well…" Jackson said.

"Well," I repeated, and we all began to laugh at the absurdity of the situation.

Darren grabbed my hand. "Let's sit on the couch."

Jackson charged forward and took my other hand possessively. "My turn, Darren."

Darren reluctantly let go of me, ever the gracious one.

I had a moment of despair as my hand dropped away from him. I didn't want to disconnect from my part-warlock love.

But then Jackson was dragging me to the couch and those feelings were temporarily forgotten. Especially when he sat down and pulled me right onto his lap. It was strange, this huge man whom I barely knew, holding me. His breath was on my hair, his hands on my waist.

But soon—too soon—I began to melt into his heat. Into the feeling of familiarity, although I'd never known such a thing before. I sighed and rested my head on his shoulder, turning over a little so I could listen to the beat of his strong heart beneath my ear. *This must be what love feels like.*

A soft growl like a contented purr rolled through Jackson's chest as his arms came around me and held me even tighter.

No one spoke, so I closed my eyes and took a second to memorize the moment. To retain what this felt like, so I could remember and cherish it for all time. When I told the story of how I met my triad of men and fell in love with them, I'd be able to tell my grandkids about this moment. About just how right everything felt. How safe I was. How warm. How aroused. *No*, I definitely wouldn't tell the grandkids that last part!

Jackson stroked my arms lazily, one hand still firmly on my waist.

I could feel tendrils of heat curling through my blood, inside my belly. Lower down, even. I felt a blush color my cheeks and I sighed, giddy, nervous, but relaxed all at once.

"So," Darren said, who seemed to be the only one able to speak to me with any sort of casual ease. "Are we as much of a surprise to you, as you are to us?"

I opened my eyes and turned toward him, not lifting my head off Jackson's chest. His hands on me were tight, and I could feel the Alpha possessiveness in him. His need to hold me, touch me.

It was thrilling to be wanted so much by such a beautiful and impressive man. What was Darren's question again? Oh, yeah... "Surprised? By the fact that there's three of you? Or that you're wolves?"

Darren grinned.

Billy even smiled.

"Well, both, I suppose," Darren answered.

I nodded. "Same for me. I never expected three... mates. And I never thought I'd marry a wolf shifter. Well..." I cleared my throat and glanced away from Darren.

"Well, what?" Darren asked.

I shifted off Jackson's lap and settled on the couch next to him.

Jackson, unwilling to give up his claim, pulled me close.

"I never thought I had anything except witch blood in me," I said. "That's what I'd always been told, anyway."

Billy coughed, clearing his throat as he moved closer and took a seat opposite us. "And now?"

My eyebrows flickered up. His voice was even deeper than Jackson's. "Tonight, after my mom magicked you all back here, she finally confessed to me that my father wasn't a warlock, like I'd been told. See, I grew up with just my mom. She told me my father left before I was born. That he abandoned her. Abandoned both of us, really, I guess."

Billy leaned forward on his chair, his brow lowered and fierce. "What was he?"

I swallowed hard. This would be the first time I'd actually said it aloud and it terrified me. "He... was a wolf shifter."

Billy gasped, his eyes suddenly wide with curiosity. "Who was he? Do you know? Is he still around?" he asked with a heady mix of excitement and intensity.

Jackson pulled me in tighter, closer to him, if that were even possible. "That makes sense. It fills in the blanks of why we want you and why you'd be our mate."

"It made a lot more sense to me, too," I agreed. "Though, I'm still kind of pissed at my mom for lying to me all these years."

"Why would she do that, though?" Darren asked, leaning forward like Billy.

"And did you get a name?" Billy added. "We should really make sure none of us are related to you."

Darren rolled his eyes. "The Fated Mates magic wouldn't be that stupid, Billy. Honestly."

I grinned at him. I liked that. "That's a cool way of looking at it. Like you guys have magic too."

"Well, it is magic of a sort," Darren said with a smile. "Even if the wolves don't want to call it that. Fated Mates is something that can't be explained in any other way, and the best part about it is that it's always right. Always perfect."

I wasn't sure I wanted to touch that one. I certainly wasn't perfect, even if they were. Instead, I looked over at Billy. "Um, to answer your question, no, I don't know who he was. I never got a name. Mom just said that he disappeared before I was born, and she never heard from him again."

A sudden, quiet stillness filled the air, the three men around me freezing as still as statues.

"When was this?" Jackson managed to ask.

"Well, I just turned twenty-two." *Like literally, today.* "So, it would be twenty-two years ago, or a little bit longer."

Jackson went completely rigid beneath my hands.

I glanced from one wolf to the other, watching their shocked expressions. Worry began to seep into my veins, dark and intrusive. "What's wrong?" I asked.

Jackson cleared his throat.

Billy stood up and clenched his fists.

I sat up straighter beside Jackson and stared at Darren. He would tell me the truth if there was something horrifying to reveal. *Wouldn't he?* "What is it, Darren?" I asked. "What are you not telling me?"

Darren ran a hand through his hair, looking uncomfortable. "There were three cousins who went missing nearly twenty-two, maybe twenty-three years ago. They went running in the woods one day and never returned. If your father was really one of those three, then you are the missing piece of a puzzle our pack has been trying to solve for over two decades."

Jackson sat up, breaking the constant contact with my body. "And according to my father, that was when everything changed for the pack."

"What do you mean?" I asked apprehensively.

Jackson turned back toward me. "Well, for one thing, ever since that night, only three females have been born to our pack. Every other birth has been a male wolf."

My mouth dropped open. Was that why I was Fated to these three? Because of something that had happened to my father? Or was there something much more insidiousand sinister going on in this town?

CHAPTER 13

JACKSON

Suspicion oozed through my mind like an inky, dark cloud. Were the witches the reason we couldn't mate within our own pack this generation? Had they even gone so far as to put a spell on us to make ensure we would die out? That we could no longer breed more wolf shifters? Such a prospect seemed too terrible, too absurd to possibly be true. And yet everything pointed to it. I opened my mouth to ask her, desperate for the truth.

Billy pinned me with a stare. His dark eyes blazed, the hint of his wolf showing in his pupil shape and the flash of yellow coloring in his iris.

It was a warning. *To me.*

When he shook his head ever so slightly, my suspicions were confirmed. My cousin didn't want me questioning our mate. Not about this topic.

She was so young and only just starting to accept our Fated Mate bond. Besides, what would Ruby really know anyway? She was conceived around the time it had all happened. She wasn't the one responsible.

But those who were should be punished.

"What's wrong, Jackson?" Ruby asked quietly.

I moved my focus to the beautiful girl who had slid off my lap and was now sitting beside me on my couch, in my home, and within touching distance. I could smell her arousal. Her need for m—for us. That was what I needed to focus on, and not the mystery of the "wolves versus witches" feud that had been going on for generations.

I shook myself and forced a smile to my lips so that she wouldn't know how deep my apprehension ran. "Nothing, sweetheart. Sorry. I just got to thinking about those three men that went missing, that's all. But I shouldn't be focusing on that. I should be focusing on you. Now, come back here."

I reached out to her, and she came into my arms willingly. Happiness soared through my veins as I pulled her safely back onto my lap. As soon as she settled, all my dark thoughts, my insecurities and misgivings, disappeared, as though they'd never even existed. How was it possible that she already affected me so much? I sighed and breathed in the delicious citrus orange scent of her hair. "God, you smell good."

She moaned softly. "So do you. How can I feel so safe and happy here with you all? After such a short time?"

Darren grinned ear to ear. "Because you're our Fated Mate, Ruby, which means you were designed for us, and we were designed for you."

"All of you?" Ruby asked, as though she couldn't fully wrap her head around the idea.

And if I were being frank, I couldn't quite either. I'd never even heard of something like this happening before. Why this one witch—who I now knew to be half wolf shifter—needed three mates was beyond me.

Darren nodded and grinned in response.

Billy just stared at her. It seemed he was as consumed and compelled to be near to her and focused on her—like she was the new moon of our lives—as Darren and me.

She turned her head and glanced up at me with her eyebrows raised high in query. "Tiffany said that wolves are notoriously possessive and wouldn't like to share a mate. Is that true?"

Talk about getting straight to the point. I cleared my throat and swallowed hard. "Well, if I'm honest, yes. We are. Our animal instincts and wolf natures are strong."

She shuffled in my lap, sitting up a little straighter. "So, you're not happy about this... relationship then?"

"Well..." How could I be honest with her about this and still keep her happy? When I didn't answer right away, she twisted around and looked at the other two and sighed. "It seems like Darren's the only one who's actually happy about us." She sounded hurt and crestfallen—lost.

And it killed me. I hated myself for not having the right answer for her.

Billy glared at me but didn't speak.

Darren jumped into the silence that hung like a blade above our heads, just waiting to fall and sever what precious happiness we might be able to have together. "It's not that they're unhappy. And I'm beyond happy, Ruby. It's just, with their stronger wolf genetics, as your friend suggested, they're really struggling with the jealous streak that makes it hard to share a mate. I think my mixed warlock genes make it easier for me, but I'm only guessing. I never thought I'd share a mate either, but I'm willing to if that's what the Fates have decided."

"The Fates? Is that what you think this is truly?" Ruby asked, her voice taking on an oddly high-pitched tone that echoed with worry.

"Well, yes. That's what we call it," Darren answered succinctly.

Ruby slid off my lap again.

I let her go without a fuss, feeling the pure anxiety suddenly pulsing through her.

"I hope you all know that I didn't plan for this," she said. "I didn't mean to make you feel jealous or possessive, or any of those things."

I frowned at her. Why was she trying to take on the responsibility for all of this? "Of course, you didn't, Ruby. This isn't your fault. It's no one's fault."

She twisted her hands in front of her, looking more nervous by the second and strangely guilty.

Did she really feel that badly about this situation? *Our* situation?

"Do you think it would be better if I just... dated one of you?" she asked.

None of us answered, we couldn't. Instead we just gawped at one another, stupefied. *Was she serious?* How would she even begin to choose?

"Which one..." I began to ask, then realized that wasn't a question I should ask or wanted answered. If we stayed together —the four of us as it was intended—for the next fifty years, I didn't want her answer haunting us.

She turned toward Darren and gestured to him. "Since Darren

is the only one who doesn't care that I'm a witch, I suppose it would make the most sense to—"

"No!"

The pained roar didn't come from my throat, like I'd expected. It came from a place to my left. *From my cousin.*

Billy was on his feet, staring straight at Ruby, his hands clenched into fists by his sides. He looked angry and defiant. But I knew that wasn't a true depiction of his feelings. He was frustrated as all hell.

I jumped to my feet too, not wanting our mate to be afraid of my cousin—one of her three men. "Ruby, don't mind Billy. He—"

Billy growled at me in warning, the sound as threatening as I'd ever heard from him. "Don't you dare make excuses for me, Jackson. It's not your place."

Ruby took a few steps forward, toward Billy.

It made me nervous. If he shifted now, he could do a lot of damage to our mate. "Ruby, be careful. He's..."

She put her hand out to me to stop me. "It's fine, Jackson," she said carefully, keeping her attention squarely on my cousin. "It's all right Billy, you can talk to me."

I took a breath and readied myself as much as I could to jump in if everything turned ugly. I would have to be faster than fast. I'd have to be super-human to save her from Billy's wolf.

Billy

As Ruby moved closer to me, my anger combined with everything else I was feeling. Jealousy and possessiveness, just as she'd said, but worse? The fear of rejection was the most prominent. It blinded me and made me feel weak—inadequate.

That was why I called out to her. To stop her from choosing

Jackson, the obvious choice. The Alpha. The strongest and very best of us. Or who she said she'd actually choose. Darren, the warlock-wolf, who was cool and calm and... a nice guy, really. I was never going to be the one she'd pick out of the three of us. In fact, I would be the last one she would choose.

She didn't know me. Hell, I'd barely spoken to her! But that didn't mean I was wrong for her, or that I didn't want her. Because I *did* want her. Despite her witch blood, and the fact that I'd have to share her with two other men forever. I wanted her more than any of that. I had to be a part of her life. I had to be with her. The mere thought of any other option ripped through me with tangible pain.

"Why shouldn't I choose just one of you, Billy?" Ruby asked me quietly.

I struggled to push forward with the conversation, through my wolf's hold on my throat. He wanted my humanity to be second to his animal control. It was often safer that way. But at that moment, I didn't agree with him. Not one bit. My mate needed to know how I felt. Verbalizing that would take everything I had, But I would damn well try.

I swallowed hard, clenching my hands so tightly that my nails nearly cut into my palms. I physically forced my wolf back down, and out of my mind. I would let him run free later tonight if he behaved now. He needed to relax, get back in his place. I was my own master. "I don't want you to choose... them." I exhaled sharply, relieved to have gotten the main message out. The rest should be easier.

Her eyebrows flew up. "You want me to choose you?" She sounded surprised

And I realized suddenly that my insecurities indeed had merit.

She had no idea that I wanted her.

I shook my head. "I don't want you to choose at all. That's not what's meant to be."

And it wasn't. I knew that with a brutal and startling clarity that shook me to my very core. If Jackson and Darren could wrap their heads around sharing Ruby, then so could I.

Ruby bit her lip. "But if I was going to choose then you'd want me to choose…"

I shook my head again, refusing to answer her question, and instead pushing forward with what needed to be said. "I want you. Just as much as Jackson. And as much as Darren. I want you, too, Ruby." My words sounded rough, like I wasn't sure how to express my feelings.

But then she smiled at me and when she did, I saw the relief and happiness in her green eyes.

And right then, a part of me melted. And I knew I would die for this woman. My mate. *Our* mate.

"I'm glad," she said. "I mean, I wasn't sure. But—"

I charged forward, all pretense and frustration gone. I grabbed her, needing to kiss her more than anything. To show her that I desired her, too. That my feelings were real and just as valid as Jackson's and Darren's. I slid my hands around her tiny waist and pulled her into me. I paused for just a moment, staring down into her huge green eyes to gauge if she was going to rebuff my advances.

Even though she'd kissed Jackson right before her mother had interrupted and blasted us back to our own town, and she'd been kissing Darren when Jackson and I had found her half an hour ago, a rather large part of me thought that she would stop me. No matter how growly or strong my wolf was, I was still afraid of rejection. And if she looked even remotely pressured or uncomfortable, I'd not only stop, but I would also leave.

But instead of looking afraid her eyes grew a little wider, as though she were surprised, and then she lifted her chin to meet my gaze and offered me her lips.

A satisfied growl rolled through me as I moved my hands up to her beautiful face, cupped her pink flushed cheeks, and kissed her. I poured every bit of desperation and love and frustration in our connection, and I was rewarded for my efforts.

Ruby kissed me back, her arms wrapping around my waist, holding me to her as she opened her mouth and swept her tongue against mine.

I groaned and lifted her up in my arms, her legs going around my hips as our bodies came together. I grabbed her ass and held her tightly to me, plundering her mouth with my tongue while marveling at the taste of her. The perfection of how she felt in my arms was everything and more.

Her hands went for my shirt buttons, and she pulled at my clothes.

I dragged my mouth away from hers to stare into her lust-filled eyes.

I didn't put her down—I couldn't— instead, I held her tighter and turned to my cousin. "Where are we going?"

"Bed," Jackson said, and charged toward his room off the living room.

I didn't bother checking with Darren. I was sure he'd be onboard anyway. I just followed my cousin into whatever came next.

CHAPTER 14
RUBY

I could barely keep my eyes open. All I could see were fireworks and flashes of white light inside my mind. My skin was on fire. Everywhere Billy touched was alight, and everywhere he hadn't yet visited was screaming out for attention.

Billy was my bad boy. Trouble. The one that ignited things in me I'd tried to ignore, and sometimes hoped weren't even there. He made me want to explore what it meant to be naughty, and he made me feel irresistible.

My bad boy carried me into a darkened room where he set me down on my feet, keeping a hand on my waist and holding me close.

I sagged against his strong body, my knees weakened and ridiculously wobbly. I forced my eyes open, though I felt drunk on pleasure, positively drugged out on one of my wolves.

We were in a bedroom. A large, dark, male bedroom. Jackson's I had to assume, since we were in his house.

This was it. It was really happening. The moment I'd been dreaming about for so long. The night I would lose my virginity and learn what true pleasure was. Hopefully.

Darren stepped into the room.

I shivered, anticipation and nervousness rippling through me. Would I make love to all three of them? And would it be all at once or individually—like taking turns? How would this work? I waited, full of nervous energy, expecting them to show me how to start, where to begin, but no one moved.

"Um, are we going to..." I gestured to the bed, feeling suddenly awkward. The heat in my blood was beginning to cool. I felt more sobered and anxious, and I didn't want that. But I wasn't going to be the one who initiated anything. I wouldn't even know where to begin!

I grabbed onto Billy's arm, desperate for an anchor or guidance. "Why has everyone stopped?"

He growled, in that soft, pleasing way. "I think we all want you to tell us that you want this, too."

I nodded, quickly. "Yes, I do. Very much. But I don't know how to—."

"You're a virgin, then?" Jackson asked, his voice deeper and darker than before.

I pursed my lips and nodded. "I am."

All three men made a strange rumbling, purring noise in unison.

I clung harder to Billy's arm. "I don't understand. Is that a bad thing?" I whispered, not quite comprehending their response.

Billy shook his head.

Darren actually laughed, breaking the intense atmosphere. "No. It's the best news any of us have ever heard," he said. "It's perfect. *You're* perfect."

A smile tugged at my lips. "Then why am I still standing here? And why are you all still fully clothed?" I was shocked I had the guts to say that, but I honestly didn't understand why we were all still standing around doing nothing. I expected to experience a whirlwind of passion, to feel swept off my feet and breathless.

They thought I was their Fated Mate, and I knew they were my true loves. My magic had called them to me and now that I had them, I didn't want to waste any more time. But they certainly didn't seem to be in much of a rush to get me naked, considering their constant and ardent declarations about desiring me. Then the spell snapped.

The Alpha took the lead. Jackson pulled his shirt over his head, unbuttoned his jeans, and stepped out of them.

I gaped at him naked, aroused and standing in the middle of the room.

Billy's hands slid down my body from behind. They moved over my waist, down my thighs, then grabbed the skirt of my new little black dress.

"Arms up," he said.

I did as he asked.

He pulled the dress up over my head and tossed it to the floor without a second thought.

I should have magicked up prettier underwear.

Then Billy made that strange, purring noise and tore at his clothes until he was naked too. Maybe sexier undies weren't really that necessary.

Their gazes were hungry as they moved over my body.

I stared at Darren, who was still completely clothed. "Aren't you going to join in?" I asked with a shy grin. I needed him to be a part of this, my sweet warlock-wolf.

He nodded but didn't say anything.

Was he going to watch? Wait until the end? Was that his plan? The questions flew around my mind unanswered.

Billy's arms wrapped around my body and pulled me into his heat.

I gasped and put my hands back against his thighs, his skin burning beneath my palms.

"Damn, you feel good," Billy groaned into my ear as he nipped at my neck and his hands came up to cup my breasts, before he began to knead them, teasing my hardening nipples

"You do too," I said, my throat tight with wanting.

Jackson walked over and knelt before me, tugging at my underwear and slipping them down my thighs.

I giggled aloud as I stepped out of my panties.

Jackson's hands came up to cup my bare ass cheeks.

I gasped at the strength of his grip; the way it made me feel owned and desired.

Then his mouth went to the juncture between my thighs.

"Holy shit!" I cried out as I reached for Jackson's head.

His tongue flicked out and caused a cacophony of pleasure to echo through my body.

My knees turned to jelly. I felt like I wouldn't be able to support my own weight much longer at this rate.

Jackson scooped me up and threw my legs easily over his shoulders, using my ass for an anchor.

I was completely exposed, my pussy open for him to devour.

Billy held my upper body tightly in his grip.

I turned my head to protest what they were doing to me, to cry out that I couldn't possibly handle so much pleasure.

A heartbeat laterBilly kissed me, swallowing my moans and gasps, silencing my protests.

Jackson pleasured me in a way I'd never even dreamed of with his lips, his tongue, his hands. They were everywhere. Inside me, on my thighs, and all over my clit that pulsed with longing. His tongue manipulated me mercilessly.

Until my back arched up and I begged him to end the torture.

Billy unclipped my bra and it fell away, my aching breasts free to the air, bare to their hands and fingers. "Let's get her to the bed," Billy said, and I was lifted and taken over to the mattress where I was laid down as if I weighed less than a feather.

Damn, it felt incredible to be manhandled. To feel tiny and delicate in their grasp.

Billy and Jackson stood over me.

Their huge, muscled bodies made my mouth water. I wanted to touch them, to kiss them, to explore each and every crevice of their raw and unapologetically sexy masculinity.

Jackson slid on top of me in one precise movement, his hot, sweaty body gliding against mine in a familiar rhythm as old and timeless as love itself.

I wrapped my naked thighs around him, my body aching for more pleasure. For the completion that I knew would soon be mine to hold on to.

Jackson stilled, then pushed up on his arms and stared down at me. "Are you protected? Or should I..."

I blinked. *What did he mean?* Then it hit me, and I blushed. "Oh. Yeah, I'm on the pill for other issues." My mother's line had notoriously terrible monthly pains and wicked irregularity, so I'd been using the pill to regulate my cycles for years now.

"Fantastic," Jackson growled as he swooped down and captured my lips with his.

I moaned into his mouth, throwing myself into the kiss wholeheartedly.

He moved his body closer, fitting us against one another like puzzle pieces that were always destined to be.

Then I felt his hard cock pressing against me, seeking, searching for the way inside my virginal body. Which was exactly what I wanted, too. I arched my back, our lips disconnecting from our intense kiss. I dug my nails into his shoulders, a gasp hitching in my throat. Was this going to hurt? Excitement, adrenaline, and desire roared through me at the thought.

"Damn, you're perfect. So beautiful," Jackson whispered into my ear, stopping any and all the worries that might invade my mind.

He pressed his hard thickness into me, so slowly, and so sweetly.

I choked on my sob as he forged his way inside of me. To feel such tenderness and care from such a huge man was humbling and revealed to me a side to Jackson I hadn't expected or really experienced yet.

There was a sudden twinge of pain but then the feeling was gone, replaced by a deep, dull ache as his body buried itself inside me.

"Are you okay?" he asked, one hand stroking my hair as he paused.

For what, I wasn't sure, but I was glad he'd stopped. Everything was overwhelming and strange. I don't know what I was expecting, or what I'd imagined, but I needed just a second to adjust. "I think so," I said tentatively. I allowed myself to relax under him, enjoying the heat and weight of his immaculately fit form. He made me feel small, protected, and desired.

He began to move his cock inside of me, slowly at first. He thrust in and out in small increments that made me gasp and cling to him; to make sure he came back every time.

Just as I began to fall into the rhythm of the new sensations, he picked up speed, thrusting harder. Uur flesh slappedtogether.

I rose to meet him, lifting my hips to greet his body with each desperate connection.

Jackson grunted and pushed even harder, seeking to plunge ever deeper.

I bit my lip, stifling the moans and sounds of ecstasy. Soon, I couldn't hold it in any longer, and whimpered as the pleasure inside my belly built to maddening and impossible heights. Everything was tightening as tingles of lightning worked all the way down to my toes. "Jackson, I—" I gasped and cried out as my first vaginal orgasm hit me.

Jackson stiffened, then thrust into me one more time.

Pulsations of heat burst inside my lower belly, my pussy spasmed, and tears leaked down the sides of my face as the beauty of the moment completely overwhelmed me. *Oh, my God.* The feeling was like nothing I'd ever known. It was an awe-inspiring perfect moment of completion.

He kissed me on the lips and withdrew slowly from my body.

And suddenly I felt... empty. Alone. It was almost painful in a sense. "Don't leave me. Please." I sat up and reached out for him with both hands. The panic was intense.

But Jackson just grinned. "What's wrong, baby?"

"I..." How did I explain the impossible sadness that came with our first time being over?

Then Billy came forward.

My heart melted. I put my arms out to him, finally understanding why I was feeling so incomplete. I needed all my mates. It couldn't be any other way.

"You aren't too sore?" he asked as he lay down next to me on the mattress.

I allowed myself to lie back down again, too. I shook my head emphatically, a second wave of desire already threatening to drown me. "No. Please, come to me."

Billy rolled on top of me and settled between my thighs as

though he'd always belonged there. He kissed my lips and stared into my eyes with so much intensity it was as though he might never see me again. Like he needed to memorize every inch of my face forever.

Jackson stood up and moved away.

I felt the weight shift on the mattress as he left, and I focused all my energy on Billy—my bad boy.

He slid down my body, kissing my neck, then stroked my breasts. First with his cheek, rubbing his roughened jaw against my flesh, then with his lips, taking the tip of one aching nipple into his mouth and sucking deeply.

I gasped and grabbed for his head, arching my back while I kept my gaze fixed on him, enjoying a perverse sense of pleasure. The image of his mouth suckling me was one that aroused me more than I thought it possibly could, sending arrows of pleasure deep into my belly.

I tangled my hands in his hair and cupped his jaw, enjoying the intense visuals and the feel of his hot mouth on me.

He moved up, thrusting his tongue into my mouth as he slid his cock into me at the exact same moment.

I groaned against his lips, my newly over-sensitized pussy opening to accept him as my insides greedily wrapped around him. He was thicker than Jackson, and he moved much faster from the start.

The fire in my belly began to build anew, higher and faster this time. I bit down on my lower lip to stifle the strangled scream that was growing in my throat and squeezed my eyes shut tight.

Billy bit my neck and sucked on the skin at the confluence of where my shoulder began. That was going to leave a mark.

I loved the idea of carrying the evidence of Billy's possession on me for all to see. I slid my hands up his arms and into his hair, holding him to me, encouraging him to mark me more. Deeper. Darker.

His breathing soon became ragged and harsh, almost growly.

Gripping him tighter, I squeezed my legs around him desperately.

He thrust harder and faster, pushing me higher, and closer toward that exquisite pinnacle of release.

I shuddered in mind-melting pleasure for the second time.

Then he came inside me, the delicious heat moving through me. Claiming me.

I moaned aloud, clinging to him so that he wouldn't leave me, too.

He joined me in mutual ecstasy, shuddering over me.

I felt a pure wave of emotion move through him. His recognition of me, of who I was and who we were together was something so much deeper than just physical.

He rolled to the side, not leaving me, but instead shifting his weight so that I was comfortable. He lifted his hand and cupped my face lovingly.

And though I knew I was red-faced, sweaty, and disheveled, he made me feel beautiful.

"Wow," he said, breathless. "That was..."

"I know," I said, smiling blissfully. If this is what the Fates had in store for me, I was the luckiest woman alive.

He kissed me softly on the lips one more time then pulled himself out of my body, leaving me cold and aching again.

I groaned. I couldn't have that feeling tormenting me every waking moment. I'd go insane!

Billy rolled away.

The pull of my magic tugged inside of me. I sat up and glanced over to where Darren sat on a large chest propped against the wall.

He was still dressed, and staring at me with a hunger that was somehow different than that of his wolf brethren.

I slid to the end of the bed and got to my feet, though my legs were unsteady.

Darren's gaze slid over my body with appreciation and when he met my gaze, purple magic swirled in his irises like whirlpools of enchantment. He wanted me, that much was obvious.

But I was covered in sweat, and the possession of my other soul mates was evident all over my body. Would he still want to be with me tonight?

"Are you going to make love to me, too?" I asked him, though the desire to cover my nakedness was strong, I resisted. Despite our intamacies, standing naked in front of these men was intimidating, especially since they were perfect specimens of what men could look like. I had no way of knowing if they liked what they saw in me. Were my breasts big enough? Were my thighs too thick? And what was Darren thinking? I wished I knew.

Then Darren stood up, a delicious and intense conviction in his movement.

My breath caught instantly in my throat. This was going to be entirely different from what I'd just enjoyed with Billy and Jackson. It was going to be something else. Somehow, I just knew it.

CHAPTER 15
DARREN

My whole body was on fire, from the tips of my toes to the inside of my gut. Part of me was afraid that if I moved even an inch, I might explode. Right here, in front of everyone. When Ruby asked me if I was going to make love to her, all that heat, all that fire, shot straight to my groin like a bullet train.

Damn it... So much for hoping to last a long time for her. I would probably come the moment she touched me if she kept on being so damn sexy. "Only if you want me to," I answered. It really was that simple and that complicated. Of course, I *wanted* to make love to her. Well, actually, to be completely honest, the animal part of me wanted to slam her into the wall and ride her well into next week. But I could see how unsteady she was on her feet, and I could only imagine how sore she would be feeling her first time.

And what if I couldn't be gentle enough? Or worse, what if I disappointed her in that very first moment when we were finally joined together? I didn't want to cast a shadow over our lives together in what should be an incredible night for us both.

"Of course, I do. Come over here." She smiled at me, curling a finger suggestively.

I took a tentative step toward her and the air around us shifted and whirled.

Billy and Jackson backed up as though they felt the magic too.

I smiled at my mate. "I have no idea what this is going to do to either of us."

She laughed, the sound musical and delighted. "Let's find out."

I reached over my head and dragged my blue tank off my body, kicked off my shoes, and took another step closer.

She closed the distance between us and reached for my buckled belt.

"Can I do it?" she asked.

A pulse of longing shimmered through me. How many things had she not done, and would she like to do to me? Hopefully as many as I wanted to do to her.

I let my hands drop away with a smile. "You can do anything you like."

She grinned then spoke a few magical words, the belt unbuckling, the zipper sliding down, and the pants disappearing onto the floor with no more than a whisper of wind.

I laughed. "Not what I thought you were going to do." I'd kind of hoped she wanted to touch me.

She beamed. "Me neither, but..." She slid closer still, running her hands up my chest, then back down again, her gaze fixed on my cock. "Can I touch you?" she asked hesitantly.

I nodded. "Of course."

Her hot little hand wrapped around me. "Wow," she whispered as she moved her fingers on my shaft, up and down, before exploring the head.

I clenched my hands into fists on either side of me. Heat bloomed inside my gut, racing down the backs of my thighs and up my back. I wasn't going to be able to handle much more of that. Her touch was like magic. I grabbed her hand and gently took it away from me, shuddering as I did so. "You need to stop that, Ruby, or I'll lose it before we even begin."

Her gaze came up to mine.

And even though I could see embarassment in her eyes she was still smiling.

"Back to the bed you go," I said, taking her hand and leading her to the mattress where I'd watched both of the other men take her in the same way. But I wanted to do something a little different.

"Kneel down on all fours for me." I guided her into the position that I hoped would give her the most pleasure. She would be able to reach her clit, or I could from this position. And it would hopefully feel completely different from what she'd just experienced with Jackson and Billy.

She frowned at me slightly.

I encouraged her into position, then stood behind her. "Damn, you're beautiful," I said as I ran my hands over her back, her hips, and her smooth, full ass. I grabbed my shaft and used my cock head to paint her pussy lips, spreading the wetness, and enjoying the feel of being an artist with the most perfect canvas.

She gasped and pressed back against me with urgent need.

My cock head slipped into her body easily and I couldn't help the moan that rippled through my chest as her delicious tightness. I considered pulling it out to spend more time enjoying her body.

Then she reached her hand back and grabbed my fingers where I held her waist. "Darren," she said simply.

My name on her lips was like a reverent prayer and made what little control I had been holding onto disappear. I threaded my fingers through hers and grabbed tight, sinking into the depths of her body with one long, strong thrust. I groaned deep in my throat.

And she met my moan with one of her own.

I'd only learned three spells as an adult and I was about to use my favorite one. I whispered the incantation and flicked my finger against her hip in a wicked rhythm to stimulate her clitoris; casting my magic around her body to arouse her in ways she likely never dreamed possible.

She gasped and pushed up with one hand, arching her back off the bed. "Oh, Darren, what are you doing?" She moaned again, more desperately this time.

I moved my fingers faster in response.

Her pussy clenched down on me.

My balls tightened agonizingly. *Shit... control. Control!* With a quiet growl I thrust in and out of her sweet, tight hole, moving my fingers while listening to her sounds of delight and pleasure.

She tightened more and more, her pussy rippling and squeezing me to unparalleled ecstasy.

I couldn't hold out any longer. Magic forgotten, I grabbed for her hips and fucked her as hard and fast I was able.

Her anguished and ecstastic cry pushed me right over the edge.

I let go, thrusting one final time and came hard. Heat swept up my back, pulsing raw pleasure through my balls, and along my cock to ripple out to every cell in my body. Exhausted, I pulled out and collapsed next to her on the bed, totally spent.

She fell to her stomach on the mattress and turned her face toward me. Her cheeks were flushed red and covered with sweat, and she was panting.

I'd never seen anything so fucking beautiful.

Then she began to giggle and grin. "I thought you said that you didn't know any magic."

I shrugged, then winked playfully, before rolling onto my back, a broad smile painted on my face. "I might have a secret or two."

She laughed and moved closer. Laying an arm over my chest, she sighed. "You certainly do, Darren."

I wrapped my arms around her and kissed the top of her head. This was unreal.

Jackson and Billy stepped forward, wanting to join us.

I squeezed her tight, realizing that my moment alone with her was over "Let's move farther up the bed." I encouraged her to shuffle up the mattress until she was laying down with her head on the pillow.

The other two wolf shifters moved in, and we settled around her satisfied body; Jackson the closest, holding her tight, me on one side stroking her sweet belly, and Billy on the other, holding her thigh. The tension in the room was minimal, considering we were all naked and vulnerable. And Ruby's once virginal body now housed seed from all three of us.

"You feeling okay?" I asked our mate, our lover.

She sighed and wriggled as though she would love to get up and run around but couldn't.

"I feel amazing," she said brightly, flashing us a brilliant, big, and beautiful smile.

Jackson grunted and kissed the top of her head. "This is only the beginning, Ruby."

I knew what he meant, wholeheartedly.

All three of us had probably not been up to our "A" game when it came to our abilities as lovers tonight. But the need to bond with her, and the sheer intensity of her attractiveness had made it very difficult to last.

The heat she imbued had certainly made me feel combustible. And I was pretty sure Jackson and Billy felt the same way.

Ruby sighed. "So true." Then she laughed. "I just still can't believe there's three of you. I can't believe this is our life—our Fate! I just can't..." She shook her head, grinning.

I glanced at the other men, and for the first time ever, felt a sense of kinship rather than the competition or the intimidation that had been there before. "You're going to be very well looked after, beautiful girl," I said. "In every way conceivable."

Sexually, emotionally, physically. We would cover every base, and be everything she ever needed, wanted, or craved.

She laughed. "If I'd known you were here waiting for me all along, I would have arrived so much sooner."

Billy growled and shook his head. "And if we'd known you were only fifteen minutes away in town, one of us would have come and claimed you years ago."

She smiled serenely. "Oh, it probably wouldn't have worked until I'd used my magic to call for you, anyway," she said absently.

And just like that our passionate evening shattered into a billion shards like a broken mirror. The potent heat and desire gone, leaving a strange chill in the air. I froze in my movements where I'd previously been tracing intricate patterns on her hot skin.

I glanced up. "What do you mean?" *She'd worked a spell to call for us?*

Ruby's eyes grew big and round, then she swallowed hard, looking unmistakably guilty.

Jackson rolled off the bed and stood beside us.

Billy withdrew his hands from her body, though he didn't leave the mattress.

"What do you mean by that, Ruby?" Jackson growled, his eyes flickering visibly between human and wolf.

"Hey," I snapped at him, suddenly alert. "Back off, Jackson."

Ruby slid up the bed, moving the pillows so she could sit up against the headboard comfortably. Then she wrapped her arms around her chest to cover her breasts, to protect her body from our view. "It isn't like it sounds," she protested, sounding vulnerable and afraid.

I smiled at her and reached for her leg, squeezing her knee reassuringly. I hated to to see her like this, especially after what we'd all just shared together. "They don't understand much about magic, sweetheart," I reminded her gently. "So, you may want to explain a little more." I was trying to sound calm and diffuse the tension of the situation, but my own magic had kicked in with the only thing I was ever good at: premonitions rolled over me. Something was about to happen. Bad or good, I couldn't tell just yet. But one thing was for sure... a shit storm was headed our way, and I didn't know that any of us were prepared for it.

CHAPTER 16

JACKSON

The witch better explain. I couldn't stop the way my wolf rose up in protest inside my head. It took all my humanity, and all my strength, to force him back down again.

Ruby needed to explain and quickly. Surely her explanation would make everything clear, and I'd find I was overreacting. I had to be. *Please,* I begged the universe. "Explain," I said more flatly than I intended.

Had Ruby seriously conjured a spell to make the three of us

fall in love with her? And if she had, how would we know the difference between our own Fated Mate attractions to her and those she had manufactured with magic? Or was it possible for her to manipulate the Fated love as well? I had no real knowledge of how potent her casting abilities were.

My anger only escalated with each passing second and the more I thought about it. My teeth clenched and my fists tightened.

"Well, ah..." Ruby shivered as though she were cold or terrified.

Darren pulled the blankets up to cover her.

I didn't know why, but that was pissing me off as well. Why the hell was he coddling her when she very well could be the reason the three of us had to share a mate? I'd just gotten my head wrapped around the idea that this was all the design of Fate. That the lack of females born to the pack meant that breeding with Ruby—bringing her into our pack—was the right thing to do. That it was what was needed and was meant to be.

Was it possible she may be just as hurtful and conniving as the witches who'd originally broke our pack? *If that's the way it went. We'd have something else to follow up on.*

Darren patted her leg. "Go on, Ruby."

She clung to the blankets that covered her perky, pink-tipped tits and bit her lip. Her eyes were wide and they kept darting to me, down and then up again. She really looked terrified—of me.

God damn it. Calm the fuck down. I took several measured breaths. "I'm sorry, Ruby. Please, explain it to us. I don't know anything about witches, really." I knew only what my parents had told me, and it was all bad. They hated the witches and warlocks in town. They said the Coven was power hungry, vindictive, and traitorous. We stayed away from them for a reason.

Ruby licked her lips. "Well, uh, I grew up without a dad. We all did... my friends Tiffany and Bella and me," she began.

"What does that have to do with us?" Billy asked, sounding offended.

I felt the same way but held my tongue. Had we landed a girl with major daddy issues?

She shook her head. "Nothing, specifically. I just wanted you to know that our past is the reason we did what we did. None of us want to make the same mistakes as our mothers."

"What? Get knocked up and abandoned?" Billy's tone was even, but his eyes flared with deep emotion.

Darren swiped out with his fist, knocking Billy across the arm with intent and more force than I'd anticipated. "Back off," he snarled protectively.

Billy growled.

But Darren held his ground and glared at him long and hard.

Billy actually backed the fuck down. Then he got up and grabbed his pants, huffing and puffing the whole time as he re-dressed.

Good idea. I grabbed mine also, feeling less exposed with my cock tucked firmly behind my zipper. "Go on," I said.

Ruby stared at Darren, her heart in her eyes. "Do you want to get your clothes on, too?"

He smiled kindly at her. "Not really. But feel free to cover yourself if you'd feel more comfortable."

A smile trembled on her lips as she closed her eyes and whispered to herself. A soft breeze swirled through the room, and then she was clothed. Or, at least from what I could see, she was. She pushed the blanket down to her waist and revealed that she was now wearing a black sweatshirt and dark jeans.

"Now, please go on," Darren encouraged her, before throwing a dirty look over his shoulder at us.

I glanced at Billy and nodded. "Let her finish." Both of us jumping down her throat was not getting us to the end of this story quickly. If anything, I could already see the wedge we were driving between the three of us, all the while forcing her even closer to the warlock-wolf.

Ruby took a deep breath, then exhaled all at once. "Okay. Long story short. On our twenty-first birthday, which was last Halloween..."

"You were born on Halloween?" Darren asked, sounding happily surprised.

She nodded.

"What does that mean?" I asked, not wanting to slow the pace of the conversation, but it seemed like I knew nothing about this world and feeling stupid was new to me. The unfamiliar ground was unwelcome, to say the least.

Darren glanced at me, though his gaze was annoyed when he did. "It's very lucky, and usually means the witch born on that day will have her powers naturally amplified."

I pressed my lips together and exhaled sharply.

He turned back to Ruby. "Which is probably why you've never known you were half wolf shifter. Normally that would reduce your powers considerably, but with a powerful mother, and the power of All Hallows' Eve..."

"Anyway," she said with another sigh. "Last year, the girls and I went away together and performed a spell that would call our soul mates to us. None of us wanted to waste time sleeping around with the wrong guys. We didn't want to endure the endless break ups, and bad marriages... you know, all that crap. We just wanted the person who was right for us, to find us. That's all."

It sounded all well and good, and her intent was innocent enough, except for the fact that she had probably messed with our entire lives. I began to pace as the thoughts whirled around my head. "So, really, you thought it was okay to use magic to call your supposed soul mate to you?" Anger tightened my gut. So, this was it, then? I'd been tricked, fooled... duped! And by magic, no less. What a fucking fool I was.

She blinked at me, hurt. "What do you mean?"

"I mean, how can you think that any of this is okay? How will we ever know if what we feel for you is real? If you're truly our Fated Mate, or if we simply got twisted up in your magical avoid-pain-plan. Your... spell."

Ruby threw back the blankets, clambered off the bed, and rose to her feet. She glared at me. "You're blowing this completely out of proportion!"

"Me?" I laughed without humor, anger settling heavily in my chest. "I don't think so, Ruby. I think it's you that's not realizing what you've actually done here."

Darren shuffled off the bed too and went in search of his own clothes, being the only still naked person in the room.

Her lips trembled and she glared even harder, her green eyes glittering with flecks of emerald. "What have I done that's so terrible? I thought you were happy about finding me!"

"I was when I thought you were truly my Fated Mate!" I was panting too hard . If I didn't calm down soon, I'd shift again. "But now, how the hell do I know if any of this is real? If it really was what Fate intended?" *Breathe. Just breathe.*

"Can't you feel it?" she cried, throwing her hands up in the air in frustration and despair. "I can! When I look at you. When you kiss me. I feel it! It's real."

I clenched my jaw and refused to answer her. I didn't know what I felt now, and I didn't trust any of my instincts.

"Jackson!" she said, her eyes brimming with tears, then she turned to Billy. "Billy? Aren't you going to say something? Anything?"

He shook his head and came to stand to my right, just behind my shoulder. We were obviously united in our questions about her using magic to influence our lives.

"I... I can't believe this," Ruby said, shaking her head as tears overflowed and spilled down her cheeks.

I tried to harden my heart against such a human trick. I told myself she wasn't upset about anything other than being found out. It made it easier to ignore her tears. Even though the wolf inside me howled in protest at my denial. If we'd formally mated with her tonight, truly given ourselves over to this woman, there would be no going back—irrespective of the fact we may have wanted to.

I crossed my arms over my chest, the ramifications of having to live with a dishonest mate plowing through me. I had to do something to deal with this unacceptable situation. I was an Alpha. I would have truth and honesty from my mate or nothing at all. "I think we need to talk about where we're going to go from here," I said. "I don't know if it's possible to undo what we did here tonight. I'll need to speak to one of the elders."

Ruby gasped in horror.

But I was already busy inside my head wondering if there was a way to reverse the bonding we'd achieved tonight. I could already sense the mating feeling building inside of me, growing like a damn flower. After I'd made love to her—no, during it—I'd sensed our connection, my wolf being willing to lay down his very life for this woman.

"Don't go, Ruby," Darren said.

I snapped my attention back to the room.

"I think I need to," she said, her voice quavering with emotion. "These two don't want me. They don't even believe that I didn't do this on purpose! I never meant to hurt anyone or play with Fate! I just wanted to find my soul mate, that's all." She was sobbing between each sentence, and each breath.

This time the wall around my heart cracked just a little. "Ruby..." I began, but I didn't know what I was going to say afterwards, and it didn't matter.

Her attention was wholly focused on Darren.

"Well, I believe you," Darren said sincerely. "I need you, Ruby, more than I need air. And I don't care if you used a spell to call out to me. I'm just grateful I found you."

A growl rose in my throat as Darren said everything she wanted to hear. The complete opposite of everything I'd said. *Didn't he realize that this could all be fake?* Our true mate, *my* true mate, could still be out there. A woman without traitorous magical blood. One I wouldn't have to share with anyone.

The wind of Ruby's magic began to whirl, and a strange white light glowed around her as if she were an angel. She looked radiant.

"I want to come with you," Darren said and reached for her hand.

She nodded and smiled at him with all the affection and intensity I'd seen in her eyes when I'd made love to her just an hour ago.

My heart broke as she glanced back at us, her gaze cold and distant. And then, just like that, they were gone.

"Holy shit," Billy said, rushing forward into the space where Darren and Ruby had been. He looked left and right like a confused pup. "Is that what her mom did to us? Just made us vanish into thin air?"

I nodded and locked my knees to stop myself from staggering for the bed. I felt completely adrift, with no foundation of strength left to speak of. "Ah... yeah, I suppose," I muttered. I changed my mind about needing to sit down. There was only Billy here to see me collapse, after all, and he was my blood, my cousin —my family.

I staggered backwards, toward the large chest against the wall that not long ago Darren had sat upon, watching us have sex with Ruby as he patiently waited his turn.

"We did the right thing, Billy. Didn't we?" I asked, dazed.

He shrugged, pacing the carpet where Ruby and Darren had stood. "Yeah, I hope so."

"You hope so?" I repeated. Didn't he know?

Billy laughed, though the sound was dark and didn't hold even the slightest hint of amusement. "You're kidding, right? If she *is* our mate, if she is the one we're meant to spend the rest of our days with, we just royally fucked up! She'll never forgive us for tonight. So, then what? We're supposed to just hang around forever without her? Not fucking likely. We couldn't endure it!"

I could hear the wolf in Billy's voice, the deep, guttural sounds between each of the clipped human words. "What do you mean, she'll never forgive us? I just questioned her magic and her motives. I had every right to. This is *my* life, Billy. *Our* lives." I heard the words, but found they were sticking uncomfortably in my throat.

Billy turned and stared at me, unspeaking.

"What?" I challenged, sitting up straighter. "If you didn't agree with me, then why stand by me? Why didn't you question her?"

"Because you're my Alpha," he said. "And my cousin."

"And I hope because you agreed with me," I shot back in heated frustration. We didn't follow the Alpha-Beta rules in our pack. And I hated to think that I'd made the wrong choice, and my cousin would pay for it.

Billy sat down on the rumpled bed; the scent of sex still heavy in the air. He shook his head. "I don't know, Jackson."

I snorted. "Well, we can fix it, I'm sure. if we find out I'm wrong... which I might not be. If I'm right, then we'll have our very own real mates just waiting to be found. Ruby's magic could have wholly fucked everything up."

Billy sighed. "I know. But if you're wrong and we *are* destined to love a half-blood witch—all three of us—do you really think she's going to forgive you after tonight?"

I frowned. "What do you mean?"

Billy shook his head and a strange smile pulled at his lips. "You really weren't listening, were you? First of all, it was her very first time, and she had sex with all three of us."

"Yeah..." *So?*

"And it was her *birthday*, today. Halloween, remember?"

My throat suddenly got tight and thick, and my words slowly came back to me like I was watching a film. I assessed everything again, from an entirely new angle, now that I was calmer. I swallowed hard. "So, tonight was her birthday and her first time ever, and I accused her of deceiving us into mating with her?"

Billy nodded. "Yeah, that pretty much sums it up."

"God fucking damn it." I stood up and ran a shaky hand through my hair. "We better go speak to some of the elders then. I need to know if I did the right thing, Billy. I have to know if my instincts were right. Or if I just fucked up our whole lives."

Billy grabbed his shirt from the floor and threw mine to me. "Let's go."

We headed out the door and made a beeline straight for the elders. If I'd let my pride—and my temper—get the better of me tonight, I was pretty sure I would live to regret it for the rest of my life.

CHAPTER 17

RUBY

The tears wouldn't stop running once I got home no matter what I did. So, I just sat on the carpet in my bedroom, wrapped my arms around my knees, and sobbed until I could barely breathe.

But Darren couldn't abide my sorrow, so he picked me up and held me on his lap, wrapping his arms tightly around me. And he kept me there until the worst of the storm of emotions had passed.

But the pain around my heart wouldn't stop. I didn't think it'd go anywhere soon.

"It's okay, beautiful girl, I'm here," he murmured in my ear. "Everything will turn out all right, you'll see."

"But how can it?" I asked him, forcing myself to look up into his face.

He wiped my cheeks with his thumbs. "Because we're meant to be together. If those stupid assholes can't see that yet, they will. In time."

My lips quivered and I bit down on the bottom one. I wasn't so sure about that. I'd given Jackson my virginity, and Billy every last bit of passion I could. I didn't have anything left to offer them. My heart was already theirs for the taking. If what I'd given wasn't enough to convince them that I was right for them, what more could I do? Wallowing certainly wasn't going to help, no matter how much it hurt. I had to be proactive. I had to do something...

I glanced up at the funky purple clock on the wall. I'd magicked us safely home to my house, and to my bedroom. It was 11:30 PM exactly, Halloween night. *I still had time to fix this!* I jumped to my feet and grabbed Darren's hand. "Come on. We've got to get out to the witch grounds before midnight."

"Where?" he asked, standing up with a slightly puzzled look on his face.

"The old church," I clarified, and turned to leave the room.

"Why?" he called out, following me as I ran down the stairs to the front door.

My mother was still out, which was good. Where she'd gone after she'd dropped me off, I didn't know. Probably Rebecca's or Kathy's. She was always with one of them, but usually both. Just like me, Bella, and Tiffany.

"I'm going to undo the spell I cast last year," I called back to him, the plan already forming in my head as I ran. I just needed the spell and some luck. I could do it, surely. Just like Darren said, I was born on All Hallows' Eve, I had naturally amplified magic! I wrenched open the door that revealed the closet under the stairs and I grabbed my mother's ancient spellbook that she hid there. The very book that had started this whole saga—where all this Fated mess began.

"If we take my car, we'll make it," I said to Darren as I tucked the book under my arm, holding it tight. I could get us there quicker via a transportation spell, but it wasn't smart to expend any more magic unnecessarily tonight. I was probably going to need every last drop of it for the reversal.

To be honest, I wasn't even sure I could do this spell by myself without my friends, but I had to try for the boys, or they'd never forgive me. And I couldn't ask Tiffany or Bella for help. Not now. It was too late. There wasn't enough time before midnight. And besides, I'd never ask them to give up their portion of the spell just because my lot had gone to hell in a handbag. They could still find their happily-ever-afters... well, as long as their soul mates didn't include two bull-headed wolf shifters!

Darren ran with m.

I grabbed my car keys from the buffet and jumped into my beat-up little hatchback, Darren close behind.

We drove along our street, toward the witches' hallowed grounds. The earth there was steeped in history and had special, sacred powers; and if there was ever a need for a boost to my own strength, it was tonight.

"Are you sure about this, Ruby?" Darren asked, his tone told me that he was worried about my sudden decision.

"Yes." I nodded fiercely. "It's the only way to prove to Billy and Jackson that I haven't befuddled Fate by putting some spell over them. They'll feel the same way after I lift it, I'm sure of it. I believe it."

Darren didn't reply.

I glanced over at him, fear coursing through me. "Unless you believe what they do, too? That my spell somehow actually managed to alter the Fated Mates bond? Made you think you could love me when you really don't?"

He laughed and slid a hand over the console between the two car seats and squeezed my thigh possessively. "Are you kidding me? I've never counted myself as lucky until I met you, but I do now! And I don't care what brought us together. Your spell, or the wolves' version of Fate. All I know is that I want you, Ruby. And if you're crazy enough to want me back, then I'm taking that as a win and going with it."

I reached my hand over his and squeezed his fingers with mine. "I'm the lucky one."

We shared a smile, then I concentrated on the road. We had about twenty minutes until Halloween was over for another year. The clock was ticking, quite literally. Then I'd have to wait another twelve months for the right night, and for the strength to reverse the spell. I couldn't wait that long. I didn't want to be without Billy or Jackson for a whole year. I wouldn't survive it. I knew in my heart what we had was real, and I was willing to fight for it.

I drove carefully, but as quickly as possible, and pulled over into the church parking lot. Dust spun up in a cloud around the car as we flung open the doors and I grabbed the spell book. Together, we hurried toward the church.

"Why here?" Darren asked.

"This church is abandoned now," I explained as I ran. "Well, for religious purposes, anyway. My Coven owns it, although it was once a Catholic church. It was built on sacred ground." I headed around the rear of the church and made my way into the graveyard, to the tree that was planted at the very center of our power.

There was no one around anymore, although I was pretty sure

that this place had been frequented all day. I looked up at the full moon and closed my eyes and focused on the waves of intense power permeating my skin and body.

"But why here? Why now?" Darren persisted, the warlock in him wanting to better understand.

I opened the book I'd carried from the car and found the page my friends and I had conjured from last Halloween. A thrill shot through me at seeing the words once more. I had to take a deep and steady breath to calm my nerves.

"It has to be here, because the power in the earth will help amplify my magic. And why now? Same reason. It's Halloween, my birthday, the very same day we conducted the spell last year!" I explained hurriedly. I placed the spell book at my feet and flicked to the next page.

Now to reverse it.

"But why do you need more power, Ruby?" Darren asked, and once again, I could hear the worry in his voice.

I closed my eyes and raisesd my hands out in front of me. I was lucky that Darren wasn't trained in the art of magic, or he would no doubt realize that this spell was too much for me alone. "Because last year I had Bella and Tiffany with me to carry some of the weight of the spell. This time I'm doing it on my own. It's all me. Now *shhh...* I need to concentrate."

Raising my voice to the night sky, I began to chant until the wind around me picked up. I opened my eyes to witness the spell book rising off the ground in front of me, open to the page I needed, the words highlighted magically for me to read.

The magic of Halloween coursed through me from the ground up. I felt the earth move, heat, and strengthen me. I began the spell to reverse what I'd done last year. And it wasn't easy. I was asking the laws of attraction, of Fate, and of love, to no longer be in play. I was actively asking them to step away. To let go of what magic they'd already worked for me.

Last year, I had yearned for this spell to give me what I needed. Now, my heart was full to the point of breaking. I couldn't have this magic be the only reason my men stayed with me. They had to love me on their own. It was the only way any of us could truly know how we felt. And what was right mattered more than even the possibility of losing them.

Tears coursed down my cheeks as I said the spell in reverse, uttering it from the last line to the top. Pain charged through my body, starting from the soles of my feet, weaving up through my legs and into my core—like a poisonous vine climbing up through the earth and spreading it's coiling branches within my body. I wouldn't give up. I couldn't. The spell was seeking payment for what I had taken, and I would give it in my blood if that's what was needed.

My gaze clung to the words, to the lines on the page. I had to finish it no matter what. My arms shook with the strain, my back cramping up as I tried to remain standing upright. The pain soon blossomed from an unbearable ache into something much more tangible and sharp. Fire, like a raging inferno, lit up my muscles, and my belly heaved as my body rejected the spell I was trying to cast.

I groaned and retched, but still the book managed to stay suspended in the air, somehow helping me finish what I'd started a year ago. I didn't want to give up. That simply was not an option. This was the only way I could prove to my soul mates—to my men—that what they felt for me, and me for them, was real. *It truly was Fate!*

The pain raced down my arms, then seared up my spine, and would soon reach my head.

Darren was calling out to me, but he couldn't reach me.

Even behind my barely open eyes I could see the white light of All Hallows' power, feel the unnatural wind swirling all around me. I was enveloped in magic. And there was only one line left.

One line of the spell to finish—to fix what I'd done. With all the strength I had left in my soul, and with my very last breath I uttered those few words, falling to my knees on the final one. And then everything went black.

~

Darren

WATCHING Ruby conduct her spell was one of the scariest things I've ever seen. My mate... my powerful, beautiful woman, surrounded by a magic vortex that had swirled around her like a tornado. It held me at bay while she'd conducted her spell, then as I was just about to charge into it, uncaring of what it would do to me, it dissipated.

I raced forward and dove as Ruby fainted, my heart leaping into my throat. I reached out and barely managed to get a hand under her head before she hit the ground.

"Ruby? Ruby! Wake up."

She didn't stir.

I swung her up into my arms and glared at that huge tome of a spell book we'd lugged out here. I was tempted to leave it on the ground, lifeless and dark, in the dirt.

But I knew that Ruby would be furious when she woke up, and the warlock part of me recognized an ancient, powerful spell book when I saw it.

So, I grabbed the book and put Ruby in her little car, then drove us back to her mother's empty house. Luckily the front door was unlocked when I tried the handle, and I brought Ruby straight in and lay her on the couch.

Then I sat on the worn-out love seat opposite the couch, staring at my mate, and waited for her mother to come home. Or for Ruby to wake up. Whatever came first.

I watched my beautiful mate and felt sick to my stomach. I should have found a way to prevent her from doing that spell. I should have convinced her that I would be enough for her. But deep inside, I didn't feel like I ever would be. She'd always miss Billy and Jackson, and I needed to do everything possible to make sure she had her heart's desire.

The front door opened suddenly and female voices chattering away burst into the silence surrounding me. Ruby's mother was home with her two friends.

I jumped to my feet, my heart pounding against my ribs. Part of me wanted to run away, but I forced my feet to stay put, to deal with whatever came out of this moment.

The three women stepped into the room, smiling and laughing together.

Then the laughter stopped.

"What the hell are you doing in here?" Ruby's mother growled at me, her eyebrows drawing together.

I indicated to Ruby, lying unconscious and supine on the couch. "Well, ah…"

The atmosphere switched instantly to one of concern.

"What happened to her?" Ruby's mother asked as she rushed to kneel beside her daughter. She put a hand to Ruby's forehead and looked at both of her palms as though inspecting the lines. Then she gasped. "She's in a magical sleep."

Ruby's mother, who looked uncannily like my mate, jumped to her feet and scowled at me, hands on her hips. Obviously, the red hair and temper ran in the family.

"What did you do to her, wolf?"

I'd never heard the word *wolf* used as an epithet before.

I swallowed against the feeling of being overwhelmed, bullied by a woman with red hair and fiery green eyes. "I didn't do anything. Ruby wanted to conduct a spell and I went with her."

"Where did you go?" she demanded.

"To the church."

There was deathly silence as the three older witches looked at each other.

Ruby's mother lifted her gaze to me, swallowing hard, her eyes shadowed with worry. "And what sort of spell did she cast?"

I inhaled sharply. "You don't know what they did last year?"

"Who?" one of the other women asked.

"Ruby and her two friends..." I began to tell them, then found my instincts flaring up saying to stop. I flicked my wrist. "Doesn't matter. Anyway, Ruby said that she and her two friends cast a spell that would make their soul mates find them. And when she told us about it tonight, Jackson flipped out and Ruby decided she wanted to undo the spell."

Her mother's eyes had gotten wider and wider, then she turned to her friends. "They did what? Holy shit on a stick... what are we going to do?"

"It's not a bad thing, is it?" I asked. "Surely..."

A cold dread washed over me as the witches turned to me.

Was Jackson right? Had Ruby and her friends messed with Fate? Or had they done something worse?

I glanced down at Ruby, lying unconscious on the couch.

Her mother bit her lip, tears forming in her eyes. "That spell is banned for a reason. It has brought heartache to anyone who's ever performed it, and it's an extremely difficult spell. I don't even know how the girls managed to pull it off in the first place."

I knew the answer to that. They'd used their birthdays, Halloween, and the pure strength of three witches who didn't want to be abandoned by their husbands the way they had been by their fathers.

But I didn't say that. Not here, to the three women at the core of their daughters' problems.

I only wanted to know one thing. "Is Ruby going to be okay, Mrs...."

"Uh, it's Sherie." Ruby's mother answered, but she didn't respond to my actual question, instead going back to assess Ruby on the couch once again, and then the three older witches began whispering amongst themselves.

I collapsed onto the love seat, my throat tight and my heart breaking. How cruel a world would it be to both find my mate and lose her in the same week?

CHAPTER 18
BILLY

We went to find Jackson's dad to ask him some questions, and we'd located him in a casual meeting with the elders.

Our news turned the meeting on its head.

"What?" Jackson's dad demanded, his temper flaring instantly.

Jackson glanced over at me.

I just stared back. I wasn't dealing with these guys. All three of them were Alpha born and my wolf didn't like going up against them.

"Our mate is..."

"What do you mean, *our* mate?" Tony demanded, one of the other elders. "It's impossible for a woman to have more than one mate. It's... unnatural. Wrong. An abomination to the order of things."

I looked away so they didn't see my anger at that statement. There was nothing abnormal about our love for Ruby, nor hers for us.

Jackson went on. "Billy, Darren, and I all feel the same way about her. And believe me, I wish it wasn't true, but it is. We *all* feel the Fated Mate attraction to her."

"Then something must have gone terribly wrong!"

Jackson swallowed hard. "We think Ruby is actually half wolf shifter. Her mother told her that her father disappeared twenty-two years ago—before she was born."

Silence filled the room as the men looked at one another.

"The Manterri cousins," Jackson's grandfather said ominously.

"Those fucking witches!" Tony seethed. "I knew they did something to our men. No wonder our pack is dying out now."

"Calm down," Jackson's dad reasoned. "Our pack is not dying out. We have dozens of strong men. This is simply an opportunity to breed with other packs. To strengthen the purebred lines by introducing new blood."

Jackson glanced over at me, his jaw tight. "I don't want to share a mate," he managed to say.

My heart sank. I thought my cousin had wrapped his head around the idea of sharing Ruby with us. Didn't he realize that we would be a bigger, stronger family with her at the center? She'd be the radiant moon of our eternal night.

His dad looked at him. "You won't have to, son. The witch's

magic won't work on you, not forever. We'll find you a wolf shifter mate, even if it means we need to travel further than the local packs. We'll make this right, boy."

I had to ask, to say something. I pushed my Beta wolf's natural submission away and forced the words from my throat. "But what of the mating bond? What if we bonded with Ruby tonight? How can such a thing be undone?"

Jackson turned to glare at me. "She cast a spell to make us fall in love with her, Billy. Surely that sort of bond can be broken."

"She *what*?" Jackson's father asked, his tone strained.

Jackson gave a quick rundown to the elders about what Ruby had said, and three of the elders exploded with anger.

I backed away toward the door and waited for Jackson to calm them down. If my stupid cousin was in denial, I didn't want to hear any more of this crap.

Finally, the growling and shouting about magic and witches died down, and Jackson began to back up toward the door. "Thank you for your time. I knew you'd have the answers," he said.

I tried not to roll my eyes as I inclined my head and followed Jackson out the door.

He marched back toward his house at speed.

"You know the elders are biased, right?" I called out to Jackson as I lengthened my stride to keep up with him. I didn't want to go back to my own bed in my parents' house, not when all I felt was turmoil and frustration. I'd rather sleep on Jackson's couch than be anywhere else right now. *Why was that?*

Unfortunately, I knew the answer. I'd mated with Ruby tonight, and therefore had bonded to the men she was mated to, as well. My home was now with the four of them. With Ruby the witch, Jackson the Alpha, and Darren the warlock wolf.

"They told us the truth," Jackson grunted. "That's more than what we got from her. And I was right. There's no such thing as three mates for one woman. We've been duped, cousin."

I sighed as I walked alongside him. There was no reasoning with him while his pig-headed, blustery Alpha was in control.

We entered Jackson's house and he went straight for the refrigerator and beer.

"You want one?" he called out, already grabbing one for me.

I shook my head. I still hadn't recovered from our drinking session a few nights ago and despite this being one of the most stressful nights of my life, it was also one of the best. I wasn't joining him in commiseration drinks. I wanted to be sober and feel everything, the good and the bad. "Nah. I'm okay. I think I'll just go to bed. You still all right if I crash here?"

Jackson took a swig of his beer and nodded absently. "Yeah. But you know there's three bedrooms upstairs. I've set one of them up for visitors. You don't need to sleep on the couch. Help yourself."

I frowned at him. Visitors? Weird. Since when did he get visitors? "Okay. Thanks." I took a step toward the staircase. The ground shook. "Whoa." I darted for the banister, grabbing onto it as the whole house rocked on its very foundations.

"Earthquake," Jackson declared, gripping the countertop for stability.

I braced, waiting for another tremble. But nothing happened. "Damn." I ran a hand through my hair and shook myself. "What the hell was that?"

"I don't know, but—" Jackson clamped his hand suddenly over his heart and grimaced, gritting his teeth as though in pain.

I inhaled sharply, finding it harder to breathe. "What's happening? This isn't normal." *Something was wrong.* I met Jackson's confused gaze. "Do you think something's happened? With Ruby? Or Darren?" I asked, panic rising within me.

Jackson straightened up with a belligerent set to his jaw. "What do I care?"

"What do you care?" I repeated with a growl, getting to my feet so I could squarely glare at my pig-headed cousin. "You're not serious, are you?" *He couldn't be.*

Jackson frowned. "Billy, what you're feeling isn't real. It's just a spell. It's a lie."

I shook my head, my wolf tearing up inside me hard and fast. Something was wrong. *Very wrong.* I could feel it. Ruby was in trouble. "Ruby needs me. I'm going." I charged for the front door.

Jackson grabbed my arm, halting me. "Stay here. There's no reason to chase after her. She's not our mate. Not mine, not yours. She's just a witch, Billy."

I could feel the command in his words and my wolf wanted to submit to my Alpha. *No.* I wrenched my arm out of his grip. Not today. Not when Ruby could be in real danger. "Get this straight, Jackson. I don't care if she cast a spell on us. And I don't give a flying fuck if what I'm feeling isn't real. It feels like it is! And there are only three wolf shifter females of breeding age in the whole pack, cousin, so although you may get one of them, I sure as hell won't."

Jackson winced.

I knew none of the three available females were his mate. He'd never shown interest in any of them past a night or two in his bed.

"Yeah, see? You don't want any of them, do you?" I challenged. "Your father and all the other Alphas have their heads in the sand about this problem. Grandma is right. We either group up or breed outside the pack. Or both! Otherwise, we're going to live out our lives alone. A week ago, I thought I was okay with that. Now... I'm not. And if Ruby will still have me, I'm going to beg for forgiveness and hope she's gracious enough to give it."

Jackson frowned at me; conflict clear in his gaze. "You can't do that."

Once again, I felt the weight of his command on me. But I laughed at him. I actually laughed in his damn face, just as Darren would have. "Get over your ego, Jackson, and your pride while you're at it, or you're going to end up miserable and alone. I'm going to get our mate with or without your help. So, are you coming or not?"

I could see the warring emotions on his face, the worry, fear, and ego fighting one another. Then finally Jackson shook his head. "No. No way."

Stubborn idiot. I shrugged. "Fine by me." IWith my keys in my pocket, I jogged out the front door, ran all the way to my place, and jumped into my truck. It was late, well past midnight, now, so if nothing was wrong and Ruby was simply asleep, I would wait in the truck until morning. I wouldn't leave her side again. And then I would beg for forgiveness.

If something was wrong... I might need to beg for more than that.

Darren

I GLARED at Ruby's mother from my place on her sofa. "For the last time, I am not leaving," I repeated, for what felt like the thousandth time.

Sherie lifted her hand.

I growled in my throat. "Don't even think about it." If she dared to transport me home again, I would only return. Again, and again. As many times as it took for the damn message to sink in. *I wasn't going anywhere.*

She looked me squarely in the eye, seemingly taking my measure. Then she nodded and went back to reading the ancient book that Ruby had been casting the spell from when she passed out.

After being unable to rouse her with any of their magic, Tiffany's and Bella's moms had gone home for the night. There was nothing more they could do.

I began to pace the living room, hands behind my back. "Could Bella or Tiffany help, do you think? They were, after all, part of the original spell from last year."

Sherie bit her lip, deep in thought. "If I can't find a way out of this by morning, then I'll contact them. But I don't want to endanger them if it's not necessary."

"I still don't understand why this was dangerous," I said. I knew only a little about magic, and this was well outside my sphere of knowledge.

Sherie sighed and looked up at me. "Because Ruby didn't have the magical ability to perform such a powerful spell on her own in the first place. I'm amazed they managed it at their age at all. But to take it back, to take that energy in on herself...? That would take more power than the original spell, even. And she didn't have it." Tears welled in her reddened eyes.

I swallowed hard. This was bad. "So, what are you saying? Does that mean she won't come out of this?" I gestured to where Ruby lay magically comatose on the sofa. Had the spell seriously leached her strength? Like, *all* her strength? As in... would it eventually wear her down and take her life? I didn't have the courage to ask Sherie straight out. Even thinking it was unbearable.

A tear slipped down Sherie's cheek.

My heart broke at the sight—a mother lost, and out of options, dutifully keeping vigil over her only child.

"It's possible," she said, a quiver to her voice. "It's definitely possible. This was big. Far too big. It was too much..." she trailed off, stricken.

I couldn't stand it. "No. That cannot happen." I argued. I refused to believe it.

Sherie sobbed, no longer able to hold back the floodgates of her emotions. She closed the book on her lap as she leaned forward, finally consumed by tears. "Yes, it can." She whispered as she placed a hand over her mouth to stem the sobs.

I shook my head, frustration and impotence making my muscles shake. "No. No! We need to do something. Anything." All I could think to do was to take her back to the church yard. To where her magic had imploded and ask whoever was out there and responsible for this, to give her back to us.

"You can't do anything," she choked, drying her eyes.

I stared at Sherie, then at my mate. "Yes, I can." I said resolutely. I walked over to the couch and scooped up Ruby with ease. "Let's take her back to the church. I'm sure the power there will help her." I had to do something. I wasn't just going to sit here and watch my precious mate fade away. I wouldn't.

Sherie jumped to her feet. "It's the middle of the night."

"I don't care." I carried my witch to the front door and nodded toward it. "Open it up, please."

Sherie hesitated momentarily uncertain then did as I asked, probably assuming I was doing this with or without her.

I stepped out into the cold night air.

She ducked around me and hurried down the driveway for her own car, then opened the back for me to put Ruby inside across the bench seat.

Another truck pulled up outside Ruby's house. One I instantly recognized.

Billy jumped out of the vehicle and when I glanced to the other side of the truck, there was no one.

"Where's Jackson?" I called out as I carefully lifted Ruby into the car.

Billy jogged over to me. "He's not coming." He frowned at me and looked over my shoulder at our comatose mate. "What the hell happened?"

"Get in and I'll explain." I jumped in the back of the car with Ruby.

Sherie slid in behind the steering wheel and glanced over at Billy in the passenger seat. "So, you're one of the three?"

Billy nodded. "Yep. I'm Billy."

"Sherie," she said, and the introductions were done.

We took off to the churchyard and Billy glanced over his shoulder, a look of worry on his face. "What happened?"

I stroked Ruby's magnificent red hair where her head lay in my lap. Her skin was even paler than normal and frighteningly cool to the touch. She was fading fast. "She reversed the spell they cast last year."

Billy's mouth dropped open. "But... why?"

I glared at him. "What do you mean, why? You know exactly why! To prove to us, and to herself, that we want her because she really is our Fated mate, and not just because she put a spell on us."

From the look of unmuted shock on Billy's face, I was pretty sure he still felt the same way I did—totally and utterly mated to her.

"How'd you know to come here, anyway?" I asked.

Billy grimaced. "Something strange happened when I was at Jackson's. The whole house shook like there was an earthquake or something. It practically knocked us on our asses."

"That was Ruby, or moreover, the effect of her spell. You should be completely cured of it now if it was the reason you wanted her," Sherie said.

I glanced at Billy.

He looked right back.

"Well?" I asked him, lifting my eyebrows with a mocking grimace of a smile on my face. "Feeling cured?"

Billy turned back around, ignoring my verbal jab, his face hard. "What do we need to do to wake her up?"

Sherie turned the car onto the gravel road that would take us to the church and shrugged. "Ask Darren. This is all his idea. I have no clue what we're going to do when we get there."

Billy waited for further explanation.

I didn't answer, I just clung to my mate. I didn't know what we were going to do when we arrived, but I knew we had to do *something* before the sun rose again and this Halloween night was officially over; taking any and all chance of saving Ruby with it.

JACKSON

After Billy left, I couldn't sleep. I couldn't even finish my damn beer. I paced my large, empty house, feeling sick to my stomach, my father's words whirling around in my head like a maelstrom.

He'd said that it had to be the magic that caused the three of us to want Ruby. That it couldn't be real. That it was impossible for all three of us to mate with her, love her, and want her.

But damn, Billy wasn't wrong... it sure as hell felt real. I missed her so much that my heart hurt. My ribs felt like they were crushing my lungs, trying to squeeze the life out of me. I could barely breathe. I shook my arms and growled out my frustration. Maybe I needed to shift and go for another run. That usually sorted me out. But two in one night? That would be a first. *Nothing else to do.*

I began to strip, feeling the unstoppable and irrepressible urge to go. To shift. To escape the incessant voices in my human mind telling me that I was going to regret my decision tonight. That Ruby was my truly mate... My wolf missed her.

I dropped to the ground and let my wolf take over, his massive body ripping through mine. Fur sprouted through my skin, and my eyesight turned to black and white night vision. I growled loudly, feeling the prickle of premonition on the back of my neck. *What the hell?* I had to go. Now. I ran for the back door, bursting through it, and headed for the woods. From there I followed my nose and went straight to town. When I reached the edge of town, I sniffed the air again. My wolf bristled.

Wrong way. Keep going. I turned toward the woods once again, and in the direction of the church; the hallowed grounds of the witches' Coven. But why would I need to go there? Would I be lured into a trap? Put under another spell? Was this how the three cousins went missing those twenty-two years ago? Were they called to the sacred place of the witches only to fall prey to their enchantments?

Despite my misgivings and worries, I followed my heart. Every instinct in my wolf body told me where I needed to go. When I finally arrived, my paws slid to a halt on the gravel parking lot. There was a single car there but no one around. I stalked closer to the large family sedan. It wasn't a car I recognized, but the scents around the vehicle, were very much familiar to me.

Billy. Darren. Ruby. And another.

I crept around the car and followed their scents, my heart pounding in my chest. I refused to step into a trap. The witches would not get me. I was no one's prey. But then I saw them, out in the middle of the graveyard, surrounding a large tree: *my family.*

I pushed my legs to greater speeds, closing the distance between Billy and me before he even noticed my presence. As I skidded to an inellegant stop, and shifted back without thinking; wanting to be able to speak and communicate with them, to find out what was going on. I rose up out of my animal state, standing on my two legs once again, naked as the day I was born.

A shocked gasp came from my left. "Do you mind?"

I glanced down to see one of the older witches that we'd met earlier in the night, glaring at me while she kneeled next to Ruby. She snapped her fingers, and I was suddenly wearing jeans. Faded, ripped, old, comfortable jeans.

I couldn't help smiling at her in gratitude. "Thanks."

Ruby lay on the ground, eyes closed, red hair fanned out around her. She wasn't moving.

"What the hell..." I dropped down to my knees in the dirt and grabbed Ruby's hand. "What happened to her?"

The woman kneeling next to her had to be Ruby's mom. She had the same red hair and a similar green angry gaze. "She reversed the spell she cast last year to appease you, and it almost killed her. Happy now?"

Fuck. Her words shot through me like molten bullets. I reeled back, pain pounding through me. "What do you mean?" I jumped to my feet and whirled around. "No. That's bullshit. She can't have. I still feel completely in love with her."

Darren took a step toward me, his eyes blazing in the darkness. "Yeah. Funny that, huh?"

I frowned at him. "So, this is all my fault?" It was. Of course, it was. She would never have attempted to reverse the spell if I hadn't questioned her motives—if I hadn't accused her of trying to manipulate Fate and our very lives.

The men around me didn't respond.

But I felt the crushing weight of responsibility fall heavily on my shoulders. "I didn't mean to hurt her. Not like this." I couldn't believe it. Had she really lifted the spell for me? To prove our love was real? "Why'd she do it?" I managed to ask, needing someone else to give voice to the thoughts plaguing me.

Darren crossed his arms over his chest. "To give you the choice. To ensure your free will. Taking the spell away would prove that it wasn't the reason you wanted her. She was trying to show us that we are actually meant to be together."

Heat prickled my eyes and my throat strained with emotion. "Really?"

"Yeah, really."

Ruby had neutralized the spell, but nothing at all had changed.

I still wanted her with every fiber of my being and my wolf still considered her his mate. Was that because we'd already mated that first time? Perhaps that was what was irreversible? I shook myself. To hell with it! I didn't fucking care anymore. This woman had sacrificed her wellbeing and risked her life just so I didn't feel trapped.

You idiot. I inhaled sharply against the pain and the feelings of betrayal that I'd caused. Then pushed the guilt aside. Recriminations would have to wait. I had to focus on Ruby. She's all that mattered now. "What can we do?" I asked the group, plaintively seeking their guidance. *My Alpha be damned!*

"We don't know," Darren said.

I walked toward Ruby's mother. "Can you use us?" I asked.

She stood up. "What do you mean?"

"I mean..." What *did* I mean? "I know nothing about magic, but it's still Halloween, technically. At least until the sun comes up, surely it still counts? This is a church on hallowed grounds and you have three wolf shifters who love your daughter and are willing to die for her. Can't you work some sort of spell to coax her back to us?"

Ruby's mother looked from me, to Darren, and to Billy, then back again. "You don't mean…"

"We do," I stated, as the other two men rushed up to stand beside me, their silence a sign of their willingness to do anything for Ruby, just as I now knew I would. "Take whatever you need from me. From *us*. Just bring her back."

Ruby's mom searched my eyes for whatever answer she was looking for, then finally nodded. "All right. The three of you surround her. I'll see what I can find." She picked up a book from the ground and began flicking her hands around and speaking in a language I didn't understand.

Lights erupted around us, floating in the air, giving us all the ability to see.

The book lit up, the pages flipping by themselves now.

I turned away from the witch mother and stared down at my mate. She was as pale as milk, her lips as red as Snow White's. My heart squeezed tight, and my knees trembled beneath me. *What have I done?*

"Okay, I think I've got something," Ruby's mother announced. "I don't know if it's going to work, or honestly if it will harm you three, but are you willing to try?"

Darren and Billy looked at me, their jaws set. They nodded as one.

"Yes," I answered for all of us. "Do whatever you can. We're in this together. No matter what."

She began to chant, and the wind picked up, whirling around us as if it were alive.

I couldn't see anything in front of me, nor any changes in

Ruby, but prickles of awareness moved up my spine like ants marching relentlessly up a hill.

Darren flinched.

Billy arched his back.

They were experiencing the same strange magical torture as well.

I closed my eyes against the pain that began to thread through my body like a needle and thread piercing my flesh, weaving up the backs of my legs, until it reached my spine.

Darren cried out in the haze of darkness and light, collapsing to the ground with a resounding thud.

I wanted to reach for him. To pull him up and take some of the pain for him. But he was too far away, and from what I could tell, he'd already passed out. I squeezed my eyes shut and clenched my hands into fists. The magic wouldn't break me. I refused to drop. I refused to fear it any longer. I would not give in. Especially not after what I'd done tonight; finding every damn excuse under the sun to try and sever the bond I'd created with my mate. And not after everything Ruby had gone through for us.

The pain moved around my waist.

Ruby's mum's voice quivered in spite of the powerful vortex as she called out. Was she still working the magic? Was the spell over yet?

I didn't want to open my eyes in case I broke something. This whole stupid mess we found ourselves in was my fault. If only I'd kept my stupid mouth shut. If only I'd thanked my lucky stars to have found a woman as beautiful, strong, and brave as Ruby.

The pain wriggled into my chest as though searching out my heart. Seeking my intentions and weighing my love. I roared at the fire inside of me, at the sheer, unrelenting intensity of it all.

Then Billy fell, the distinct *thump* of him landing next to me sounding loud in my ears.

I clenched my hands into tighter fists and hardened my jaw,

hearing my teeth crack. My heart pounded faster. I wanted to vomit. To give in. To open my eyes and see if I could make the pain stop. Sweat rolled down my forehead but I refused to let up. *Pain is only temporary*, I reminded myself. *But Ruby is forever.* I opened my mouth, desperately panting for breath.

The witch's voice continued to call out, louder and louder seemingly commanding the very earth itself to hear her plea. If any of it was in English, I didn't understand a word of it.

Blood started to pour from my nose, and ran over my lips. The metallic taste spilled into my mouth, and I shut my lips against the familiar tang. I swayed on my feet, then locked my knees by sheer force of will, to stop myself from falling. I wouldn't give in. *I wouldn't...*

And then it stopped, like someone just switched off a tap.

I went from spilling blood and feeling pain and prickling hot needles through my organs, to... nothing. Absolutely nothing. I was fine. My eyes sprung open, the maelstrom gone.

Darren and Billy remained on the ground in heaps. Neither moved, other than the slow rythmic rise and fall of their chests. They'd passed out hard by the looks of things.

Between them lay Ruby, blinking her lovely green eyes.

"Ruby. Oh, my God. You're okay!" I moved toward her and fell to my knees, my exhausted body finally giving out. I crawled over to her, headless of the grass and cold dirt beneath my hands.

"Jackson... what are you...?" Ruby tried to sit up.

I pulled her into my arms, unable to hold back a second longer. I kissed her head and squeezed her tight, a lump forming in my throat. "I'm so sorry, Ruby. I should never... I don't..." I buried my face in her hair and inhaled the sweetness of her scent. I couldn't speak anymore. The words didn't matter right now anyway. She was alive.

Ruby's hand came up to stroke my hair.

Around us, the others roused and padded over to us.

I didn't let go. I wasn't sure if she would ever forgive me for what I'd said tonight, but I'd beg her for the chance to prove I could change. Billy had been right all along. The Council was bigoted and biased against witches, and I had to carve out my own path now—with my new family, and the woman Fate had chosen to be my mate. *No*, I caught myself. *Our mate.*

I'd been dreaming about the weirdest things. Of wolves and a graveyard and flying. I think I'd been flying? But to where… I wasn't sure. I woke up suddenly, as though being shaken. I blinked my eyes open and lifted a hand to rub the sleep from my face.

"She's waking up!"

I heard a male voice and I gasped. *Who was that?* I tried to sit up, but my body wouldn't cooperate. "What the…" I opened my eyes fully, blinking rapidly to clear them as light poured in. Where was I? I glanced around, seeing all three of my mates, as well as my mother, all standing together. All in my living room—that was if I was correctly identifying the funky red wallpaper. "What are you guys doing here?" I asked, trying to sit up again, groaning with the strain of lifting my head.

"Here. Let me help you," Darren said, picking me up gently and sitting down so that I could lean against his chest.

I looked around at the anxious faces hovering over me.

Mom collapsed into the armchair, her hair wild and tangled.

Billy and Jackson stood nearby; their faces lined with stress.

"What happened?" I asked, then looked straight at my mother. "Mom? Are you okay?"

"Yes, honey. I'm okay," she said, though her voice trembled and there was an unmistakable sheen of tears glazing her eyes.

I glanced over at Billy and Jackson. "When did you guys get here?"

They didn't answer.

I began to feel frustrated. "Would someone *please* tell me what's going on?"

Mom jumped to her feet and frowned down at me, clearly at her wit's end. "What's going on is... you almost bloody died!"

"How?" I asked, my brows scrunching as I glanced around for a clue. "I don't remember anything."

Jackson stared at me, his eyes pools of sorrow. "What do you remember about last night?"

I frowned, searching my memory. "I came to your house..." *And we all made love.* "Then you told me that you..." *Didn't want me.* I trailed off and swallowed hard.

Jackson had told me that he didn't think I was his mate. That the magic I'd used to call him to me asking for my soul mate to find me had tricked them. He'd said that my magic had played with Fate. That what they felt for me wasn't real.

Jackson fell to his knees in front of me and crawled over the dark gray carpet, before grabbing one of my hands in his as he went up on one knee.

I stared at him. Why did he look like he was about to propose marriage or something? "What are you doing, Jackson?"

"I'm apologizing profusely for being such a jackass."

I tried not to smile, but he seemed so earnest. I knew how much it took for an Alpha to admit they were wrong. "So, you don't think I fooled you into mating with me anymore?"

My mother gasped and then flinched.

I purposely ignored her. I would deal with all the ramifications of *that* later.

He shook his head. "No. And I can't tell you how stupid I feel. That you would put your life in danger to prove to us that you're the right one for us."

I frowned. "I..." The memories came flooding back. Of me wanting to reverse the spell. Of taking Darren to the church yard, of the power and the pain I'd felt. My gaze shifted to my mother. "What happened?"

She smiled sadly. "You went into a magically induced coma, Ruby. You took too much on yourself. You know that don't you?"

I nodded, admitting to the truth. "Yes, I do. I knew the spell was too much for me, but I didn't want to risk Bella or Tiffany. They're my best friends. My Coven sisters."

"But you were willing to risk yourself?" Jackson asked, his tone accusatory.

I turned back to him. "I was trying to prove to you that I hadn't tricked you. And now you know. I removed the spell, and you're still here. So, I'm assuming it wasn't my spell that made you love me in the first place. It just helped us find eachother." I glared at the big, stupid Alpha.

Jackson grimaced and nodded sheepishly.

Mom got up wearily from her seat and yawned. "You seem

yourself again, so I'm going to bed. The sun will be up in about an hour, and I haven't slept a wink tonight. But you and I need to have a talk, Ruby. Later."

I swallowed hard. "Yes, Mom."

Mom smiled to the three men and left the room without another room.

My men gathered around me, stepping closer, becoming more protective.

I glanced up at Darren, who was holding me, but not speaking. "So, I pushed it a bit far, then?"

He kissed my hair and shook his head. "Way too far, baby. We almost lost you."

"But what brought me back?" I asked. "I'm starting to remember a little about going to church, but nothing after that. How did I even get back here?"

Darren sighed and twisted his fingers into mine. "Well, we drove back here after the church. But what got you to wake up is a whole different story. Your mother cast a spell to bring you back. She said you were in some sort of coma—that you'd drained yourself."

"What kind of spell?" I didn't know anything that was strong enough to return a person's soul after they'd gone burned out past the point of no return.

Darren answered. "I don't know. But she used us."

"*Used* you?" I repeated. Did he mean as anchors to this world? Or did she tap into their own magic? Their love for me?

Darren nodded. "Yeah. I'm sorry to admit that Billy and I passed out. But Jackson held out to the end. One advantage to being an Alpha, I suppose."

He said the words with a teasing tone, but I could hear the stress and admiration for Jackson's strength behind the words. Whatever they'd gone through together last night had not been pleasant. In fact, it sounded like it was downright horrendous, a real struggle of life and love triumphing over death.

I glanced toward Jackson. "So, does that mean that you still want me?" My gaze flicked to Billy. "You all do?"

Billy grabbed my hand and nodded fiercely. "Yes, I do. We all do."

Darren kissed my ear and whispered almost inaudibly, "Billy came back first. Then Jackson."

I swallowed hard, pain gripping my heart as I prepared myself to ask the next question. Their answer would determine so much about our future. I glanced back at Darren, the only one who'd stuck by me through it all, and the who would tell me the truth no matter what. "After they found out what had happened to me? Or..."

Billy shook his head, speaking for himself. "No, I could feel that something was wrong. Or maybe it was just my conscience eating me alive, I don't know. But I came back on my own. I had to. For you."

"And Jackson did, too, when it mattered most," Darren added. "I didn't have to call either of them. They both came looking for you."

Tears filled my eyes, blurring my vision. "You really want me as your mate, forever?" I asked, reaching out and gripping both Billy and Jackson, Darren's arms still around me.

"Yes. We do. We all do," Darren said, and began to kiss my face, then my cheek... then my lips...

Warmth swamped me and I closed my eyes, allowing myself to be dragged into the heated vortex of love that Darren, Billy, and Jackson had come together to create just for me.

EPILOGUE

RUBY

A month later.

I stared at Jackson as I slid my silk nightgown off my shoulders, letting it slide sensually down over my hips to whisper soundlessly to the ground.

"Are you sure about this, Ruby?" Jackson asked as he swallowed hard, his gaze intense as he drank me in.

I glanced around the large master bedroom and at my three men. "Yes. I'm sure."

We hadn't had sex since that first time on Halloween night, a month ago. We'd kissed and petted, and done things that made me wild with desire, but my men had patiently and nobly wanted to wait until I was fully healed before we engaged in anything more adventurous again.

And I loved them for it... but *damn*, was I desperate now—I needed them fiercely. I walked over to the huge bed we'd jammed into Jackson's house when we all moved in here a few weeks ago. It was two king-sized beds joined together, and I slept in the middle; the tasty meat in our proverbial shifter sandwich.

Crawling over the mattress, aware of their hot gazes on my naked ass, as I lay down on the pillow I'd occupied since moving in. "Please. Come to me," I begged them. "I need all of you." I wasn't sure exactly how this was going to work, but I'd been having a hazy recurring dream since the day after Halloween. Of all three men in my body at the same time. Mating with me. Completing me. Sealing our Fated connection.

There was no other word for it. I didn't feel as connected to them as I yearned to be, and tonight I would make it so. I'd been practicing my magic, and I had ways of helping them enter all of me.

The three men undressed quickly, jeans, shirts, and boots falling away in a tumbling pile of clothes. Then the three of them looked at one another.

And I saw the wolf flash in their eyes. My stomach tightened as my own wolf shifter genes, those that I was only beginning to recognize, called out to its mates.

They crawled onto the bed to join me.

Billy on my left.

Jackson on my right.

And Darren slid up the middle and lay on his belly, pushing open my thighs to stare down hungrily at my pussy.

I gasped and squirmed under his gaze, wishing the lights were off. Even now I still felt self-conscious, though I was slowly learning to accept that my beautiful harem of men loved me just the way I was.

He grinned at me and caressed the inside of my thighs with his thumbs. "Nuh-uh. No hiding now, my beautiful one," he coaxed.

Darren moved up, turning his head to kiss a trail of fire up the inside of one thigh, before licking a glistening path to my throbbing clit.

I grabbed his head and cried out as pleasure shot straight through my core like a flaming arrow.

But he didn't stop.

Then Jackson joined in, kissing my shoulder and cupping my breast.

It was too much, and I cried out again, part of me fighting the erotic assault to my senses. It was positively impossible to process it all at once.

Billy ran his hand over my cheek and lifted my face, sliding in closer to press his lips against mine. Softly. Gently.

I groaned at the feather-light touch of his kiss, wanting more. Needing him to kiss me harder. I instinctively let go of Darren's hair, reaching up instead to entwine my fingers in Billy's hair. This was what I wanted. All three of my men surrounding me, loving me, all at once. Now it was time to let go of all control and to surrender completely to the flow of the storm surrounding me.

Darren suckled on my flesh and swiped his tongue across my sensitive pussy lips.

I broke free of Billy's kiss to moan aloud, tendrils of pure pleasure swirling through my legs toward my center. "Oh, please. Come up here," I said.

But the men seemed to ignore me as Darren pulled back to stand at the edge of the bed before he grabbed my ankles and dragged me down the mattress to meet him.

I giggled at the playfulness and the smile from Darren that came with it. "You guys have this all figured out, don't you?" I asked, noting the confident and coordinated way they were moving.

Billy crawled over to suckle my nipples, the unexpected heat of his mouth taking me by surprise.

I gasped as renewed fire spread through me.

"Yep. We've been planning this for a month," Darren said.

Jackson lay on the mattress next to me, then rolled to grab me around the waist. "Jump up on me, beautiful."

I rolled with him, squealing with delight at being tossed around. My pussy was soaking wet and as Jackson's hard cock jutted up beneath me. I tilted my hips and rubbed myself along his shaft, up and down, loving the feel of him against me.

He groaned suddenly.

I looked down, catching sight of the yellow wolf in his irises.

He lifted up and pulled me down, attaching his wet mouth over my nipples as my breasts spilled over.

I moaned, arching my back and thrusting my breasts so that he would suckle harder. Fingers explored me from behind and I found myself arching my back further to encourage the contact. I glanced over my shoulder and groaned.

Darren ran his hand over my searing flesh, circling my clit, before dipping inside me.

I cried out, every inch of me filled with greed and an insatiable need for their touch.

"Hurry up!" Jackson called.

Billy suddenly reappeared, coming back from the bathroom holding a tube of something.

"What's that?" I asked, squirming over Jackson.

Billy smiled. "It's lube. You wanted all three of us at once and I don't want to hurt you."

"So, you're going to..." *Fuck me in the ass.* I couldn't bring myself to say it. My cheeks flared with color.

Billy grinned and nodded, but thankfully didn't verbalize it.

I moaned as arousal swept through me once more and a soft wind rustled my hair. I looked up to find white magic swirling in the air around us. It moved in a leisurely circle, drawing us closer and closer together.

"I don't know what's going to happen," I panted.

Darren slid two fingers into my pussy, making my body ache for more.

"Neither do we," Jackson growled from beneath me, laying back on the bed, then grabbing hold of my hips. "You ready?"

I nodded with complete trust and let my men lead me.

Jackson grabbed hold of his cock and slid the large arrow-shaped head along my quivering pussy lips, then thrust up, joining us in one single, long stroke.

I gasped, sucking in breath, as lights exploded inside my mind. He was so big, and the sensation of fullness was beyond incredible.

I panted and moaned, feeling his body quake beneath my hands.

"Lean forward," Billy encouraged, pressing on my back so that I was forced to lean closer to Jackson.

I did as he directed, exposing my bare ass to him.

Billy moved his slicked-up fingers over me, the oil running over my skin and down my legs.

I tried not to focus too much on it, instead closing my eyes and enjoying the sensation of Jackson's cock inside me, thrusting in and out.

Then I felt Darren's hand on my chin, lifting my face.

I opened my eyes and stared at where he knelt next to Jackson on the bed, his cock in his hand, outstretched and waiting for my pouty little mouth. My stomach tightened with excitement and desire as I leaned forward, my tongue darting out tolick the hot, pink head of his cock.

He groaned and thrust his hips forward.

I parted my lips and welcomed him into my mouth, exploring his hot flesh with my tongue.

Billy rubbed his cock against my asshole.

I closed my eyes, consciously sending my magic down to the tight area he was about to enter. With time, I was confident I'd be able to enjoy taking all three of my men at once, without magical assistance. But tonight, I was going to cheat a little, and use my magic to stretch me, lube me up, and dull the pain.

Billy said to me, "Are you really sure about this, baby?"

I tried to nod, but my position made that difficult. I couldn't speak with a mouth full of cock, and I sure as hell wasn't letting Darren go. A thumbs-up seemed too ridiculous of a gesture, so I just wriggled my hips a little and pressed back. *Surely, I was being direct enough?*

Billy pressed forward, his hard, thick cock plowing my ass, stretching me, and completing my trifecta.

I closed my eyes on a moan as a wave of pleasure rolled over me, drowning me alive in ecstasy.

"Fuck... I'm not going to last long," Jackson groaned from beneath me, squeezing my hips and thrusting in and out in short, sharp, powerful bursts.

I let my mouth slip from Darren's cock momentarily. "You don't have to. Please. Come inside me. All of you." My cheeks flushed with a fiery blush at saying those words, but I didn't hesitate to re-open my mouth and get back to sucking on Darren's gorgeous, hard cock.

Billy growled from behind me, thrusting harder, deeper, and faster.

My magic mercifully held firm, so I relaxed into Jackson's grip and let my men ride away with me. My body became a living conduit of my love for them, and theirs for me. I could feel the wolf inside me rise, stretch, and howl to the moon. And then there was my magic. Weaving us all together, for all time.

I gasped around Darren as he began to thrust into my mouth and deep into my throat with a frenzied purpose.

Jackson and Billy groaned from beneath me and behind me.

"I'm going to come," Jackson growled.

"Me too," Billy snarled.

I squeezed them tightly with my pussy and ass, my pleasure rising and cresting within my belly, just waiting for the moment I could plunge and join them in mutual release.

Darren tried to pull away from me at the last moment.

I grabbed his shaft with my hand possessively and held him in.

"But..." he rasped.

I shook my head and sucked him deeper into my mouth, creating a tight seal with my lips, wanting absolutely all of him.

"Oh... God!" Jackson cried out, grabbing hold of my hips and thrusting up into me.

I waited for one soundless, timeless moment, and then it began. Jackson's seed pulsed into me, and I groaned as my own orgasm raged through me like wildfire. Pleasure swept through me, and I shuddered and shook over the top of him like a leaf.

"Fuck!" Billy swore, thrusting deep and releasing his seed up my ass.

Another round of orgasmic spasms hit me, and I would have screamed in ecstasy except for fact Darren's cock was still in my mouth.

"I'm..." Darren began to shake and stiffen.

I took him to the back of my throat and valiantly swallowed

down his seed, making my body a vessel for all three of my mates at once—just like in my dream.

Finally, when the groans and gasps began to quieten, I let Darren's cock slip from my mouth and collapsed on Jackson's chest, panting and whimpering as the aftershocks of pleasure continued to rock through my body.

Billy retreated and rolled onto the bed next to me.

Jackson slipped free of my body a moment later as well.

I sighed happily, though I felt strangely empty now. I closed my eyes and reached for my men with both hands, needing contact.

With one hand on Billy, one hand on Darren, and my body resting on Jackson, I gathered and focussed my happiness and magic and sent it out in a wave that rippled over my men.

I heard a moan and two gasps and smiled. "I love you. All of you. Thank you for making my dreams come true."

The men drew closer, and I let myself drift off into that magical place between wakefulness and sleep, to just float in the love all around me.

These beautiful, sexy men were my Halloween miracle for a Halloween-born witch.

Now, it was Bella's and Tiffany's turn to find theirs!

You can download book 2:
https://books2read.com/pack-magic
Or read on for a sneak peek into...
Pack Magic

A few days before Thanksgiving.

I glanced around Kathy's lounge room, looking from Ruby to Tiffany, then back at our mothers lined up on each side of the room. I could have cut the tension in the room with a knife. Although, seeing as we were all witches, a relaxing spell would probably have been better for the stress.

"Girls, you have to understand that what you did was danger-ous," Ruby's mother began to lecture.

I stifled the sigh that rose in my chest. I knew what was coming.

We'd been called to Ruby's house under the pretense of having 'a chat' but really, our moms just wanted to yell at us for the love spell we'd cast last year on Halloween.

Sherie pushed up from the couch where she'd been sitting and moved to the front of the lounge room, standing before the cold fireplace. "Every person who has ever worked that spell has had to endure dire consequences. Just look at what happened to Ruby." She pointed to her daughter as though our friend's happiness—having found not one, but *three* Fated Mates—was a bad thing.

I wanted to refute her claims that we'd done something terri-ble, but I kept my mouth shut. I wasn't ready to jump into the fray of this lecture yet. I needed more information before commenting.

Tiffany, on the other hand, never thought twice before butting in with her opinion. "You're blaming us for what happened to Ruby?" She said as she jumped to her feet to confront our moms. "Ruby's happy! She found her soul mates. But if you really want to blame someone for us casting that spell, how about we blame you three for the fact we had to do it in the first place!"

Damn, we got there quick. I grimaced. This was not going to be pretty.

Sherie dropped down onto the couch next to my mom and their faces drained of color.

My mom glanced over at me. "What does she mean, Bella?"

All five witches turned to me.

A flood of heat coursed up my face and I felt even more uncomfortable—if that was even possible. I shrunk back into the sofa. I didn't want to have this conversation. It was one I'd avoided all my life. I gestured at Tiffany with anxiety. "She can explain," I said quickly.

Tiffany put both hands on her hips and stared down at our moms. "How can you not put two and two together? Seriously? All three of us have grown up without fathers. We've had to grow up seeing you all single and miserable our whole lives and it's been hard! We don't want that for ourselves, or our children. We want..." Tiffany stopped, her voice stuttering to a halt as she swallowed hard, a sheen of tears in her eyes as anger gave way to sadness.

Ruby wasn't moving a muscle, and I could see how close to tears she was as well.

Damn. It was my turn to speak. I had to explain and try to salvage this shitty situation we'd found ourselves in. I stood up and reached for Tiffany's hand, threading my fingers in between hers and squeezing tight. "We found the spell book a few years ago," I began. Well, technically, Ruby had, but there was no way I was laying the blame on her. "And it said that the spell would attract our true soul mates to us. None of us wanted to date anyone else except the men we're meant to marry. And after watching the three of you survive the past twenty years heartbroken and alone, we wanted to avoid that, if it was possible."

Mom stared at me; her mouth open. "But, Bella, you know how much power is required for a spell like that. It was dangerous. How did you even pull it off?"

"There's three of us," Ruby said, standing up and joining in the conversation. "We did it together."

My mom's gaze slid to Ruby, then back to me as though Ruby hadn't spoken at all. "Bella? How'd you do it?" she repeated.

I bit my lip. "Um, I just helped as much as I could."

"You mean, you shouldered more than your fair share?" my mother accused, her mouth twisting in a way that showed both concern and a measure of pride.

I shrugged and licked my lips, trying to brush the accusation aside. "We all did the best we could, Mom."

Ruby reached out and grabbed my hand, the one that wasn't already holding Tiffany's. "What did you do, Bella?" she pressed, her brow furrowed.

I shook my head. "Nothing special. The spell just required a lot more power than I'd originally estimated, and I needed to throw in a little more than I expected. That's all."

Ruby stared at me, then the light of comprehension dawned in her eyes. "No wonder I didn't have a hope of undoing the spell without you."

I squeezed her hand, offering her my support in return. "But you did! You managed it without any help at all."

She chuckled awkwardly. "Maybe, but it almost killed me."

I inhaled sharply, pain squeezing my chest at the thought of losing one of my best friends. "Please don't do anything like that ever again. You could have asked me. I would have helped you with anything you needed then, and I still would, now."

"I know, but there wasn't time. Well, I didn't think there was anyway." Ruby turned back to our mothers again. "Does that mean that Bella is going to cop more of these so-called 'consequences' for using the spell?"

I bloody hope not.

The three mothers exchanged glanced, worry clear in the lines on their pale faces.

My heart dropped. "Great."

Mom looked to me. "Not necessarily. I'm more interested in the fact that you have more power than Ruby and Tiffany. I mean, I've always known of course, but..."

"Does this have something to do with the fact that my father was a wolf shifter?" Ruby burst out, shocking the whole room into silence.

I gasped and turned to stare at her. "Seriously? When did you find that out?"

How could that be? *None of us could shift.* We were all full witches... weren't we?

"Mom told me, the night of Halloween," Ruby said, then grimaced in apology. "Sorry I haven't caught you up on that. My brain's been a bit scrambled with everything's that happened." She made a whirling signal next to her head with her fingers.

I nodded, a shiver of premonition sliding down my spine. I turned back to our parental units. "Mom..."

She gulped visibly. "Yes, Bella?"

"Was my father a warlock?" I'd been told he was, and it had always made sense that he would have been. Even now. I was more powerful than Ruby, and Tiffany too for that matter. My magic gave me the sense that I wasn't going to like the answer that was about to spill out of my mother's mouth.

Tiffany seemed to understand why I was asking and rounded on her own mother as well. "What about my sperm donor, then?" she asked boldly.

I flinched at her choice of words, but Tiffany had always used humor to deflect from anything serious or hurtful.

Mom, Sherie, and Kathy looked at each other, their eyes wide and wary.

Oh no, this was a secret they all shared, which could only mean...

"Mom," I said, adopting my serious tone of voice. "Please answer the question. Who, or more likely *what* species, were our fathers? You all led us to believe they were warlocks."

Mom waved her hands at us. "Girls, sit down, or we'll stand up. But please don't stand over us. We aren't the ones in trouble here."

I raised my eyebrows. *We'll see about that.* I tugged at Tiffany and Bella. "Come on. Let's sit."

Tiffany's barely leashed anger vibrated through the room in response.

"Let's hear them out." I tugged harder and managed to get

both of my friends to sit their butts back down onto the sofa beside me. I knew beyond a shadow of a doubt that the answer to this question was going to change the course of our lives forever. "Okay, we're listening. So, tell us," I said, clenching my teeth in preparation for what was to come.

Sherie stood up and paced to the front of the room again. "I'll go first," she said. "Because Ruby already knows about her parentage. Her father was a wolf shifter and a pure blood from what I understand; which is why I was worried that she might have exhibited signs of being part wolf when she was younger. But as it turns out, she never did, and won't now that she's reached full maturity. But when she brought home a wolf shifter for a soul mate, it made sense to me."

Sherie's lips kinked up at the sides. "I didn't expect three of them of course but considering the curse—I shouldn't have been surprised."

"What curse?" I asked, narrowing my eyes.

Sherie slapped a hand over her mouth suddenly as though she'd revealed more than she was meant to, her eyes wide and panicked.

"Great, even more secrets," I muttered under my breath.

My mom stood up, directing Sherie to take a seat. "We can talk about that later. First things first."

Mom took a deep, steadying breath and stared at me, then Tiffany. "I think the easiest way is to explain is that all three of your fathers... were first cousins."

Ruby jumped to her feet. "They were what?" She whirled on us. "Do you know what that means?" she said, her face pink with excitement and wonder. "We all have wolf shifter dads, which means we could all have soul mates from the pack! Or you guys might even have three like me." Ruby sounded positively elated by the idea and clapped her hands.

My own immediate reaction was quite different. My stomach

twisted and lurched, upset by the new revelation. How I saw myself, my genetic makeup, had been turned on its head in a heartbeat. I was part wolf shifter. I wasn't a real, pure-blooded witch. *Damn it.*

Tiffany stood up, grinning like a loon. She obviously didn't mind the idea of mixed blood. "Three wolf shifter mates sounds good to me."

I could only see one silver lining to this dark cloud. "You know what it also means?" I said to them, getting slowly to my feet.

Now our sister-like friendship made more sense than ever before. No wonder we loved each other so much and felt so connected, even though we weren't related. *Or we hadn't thought we were, anyway.*

"What?" Ruby asked, her expression bright.

"We're related," I said. "If our fathers were all first cousins, then we're officially second cousins, all of us." I'd always thought of these two girls as my soul sisters, my best friends. Now, they were more. They were literally family.

Tiffany cried out happily and hugged Ruby and me to her.

I let my cousins, my best friends, hold me tightly, but inside, my heart was aching. I felt betrayed. My mother had lied to me all these years. I had wolf shifter in my blood.

A rough cough made us break our embrace. It was my mom.

"I'm glad you're all happy about your relationship because it's a very special bond,even without the blood link. We always believed that the three of you were meant to be. Your linked birthdays meant that you were supposed to be born together."

"But...?" I led her to continue. I had a feeling there was more to it.

Mom smiled at me. "But your father, Bella, *was* part warlock. He was related to..." She desperately glanced at Sherie for help.

"Darren," Sherie offered.

Ruby's mate! The one with one quarter warlock genes, and three quarters wolf shifter.

"Yes, thank you. Darren, I believe," Mom finished.

Ruby looked at me. "Really? Well, that's kind of cool. Our kids are going to have all sorts of crossed over relationships at this rate."

I swallowed hard. We weren't finished yet. "So, tell me the real story of my father then. Did he actually abandon you like you always said?"

Sherie stood up next to my mom. "All three of us were dating your fathers in secret. We knew the Coven wouldn't understand. The high warlock hated the wolf shifter packs in the area. We weren't allowed to go anywhere near them."

"Then how did you even meet?" I asked. Then I waved my hand. "No. Forget that part. I don't care." I shook my head, angry. The details didn't matter. What mattered was that everything I'd been told all my life was a damn lie. "So, you were actually dating my father. You weren't abandoned by some random stranger?" I lashed out. Which in retrospect was a much better tale and made more sense as to why my mother had never dated anyone else.

My mother shook her head slowly. "No. I was totally in love with him. He was half wolf shifter and half warlock. His mother was a witch the pack had taken in, so I don't know why our high warlock hated wolf shifters so much when they seemed to be accepting of us at the time."

I filed that piece of information away for another day. Maybe the witch who'd married the shifter all those years ago had been related to the high warlock? Or was meant to marry him and chose a shifter instead? Who knew at this point? They were all gone, or dead. I wouldn't be able to ask them.

"So, what happened? Why did they disappear?" That seemed to be the most pertinent part of the story for me. I wanted to know what had happened to our fathers. All three of them.

Tiffany grabbed my hand. "Hang on. Can we back it up? Can I just ask if my dad's a half warlock too?"

I smiled and nodded, but I already knew the answer. There was a reason I was more powerful than Tiffany and Ruby. It was because of my father's mixed blood—he had the most warlock in him.

Tiffany's mom turned to her. "Your dad was a full wolf shifter, honey. Similar to... Billy, I believe. He was Ruby's father's Beta."

The spell and the people involved were all turning full circle. Our three fathers were just like Ruby's triad: two full wolf shifters and a half breed. Now Tiffany and I had to wait to see what men were sent our way. Would we get three as well? Or just one?

My stomach clenched. I wasn't sure I could handle three. That seemed... unmanageable. I still wasn't sure how Ruby did it.

"And you two dated as well?" Tiffany asked.

Tiffany's mom nodded, though her cheeks flared red.

"Mom!" Tiffany said. "Don't lie to me."

"I'm not lying!" Kathy retorted earnestly. "It's just that we'd only just started dating when he disappeared. And I conceived you the very first time we slept together, so I always felt like you were meant to be, Tiffany. Always."

Tiffany slumped toward the couch.

I sighed. There was just too much information coming at us. Too many emotions. And yet I couldn't stop now. I needed to know everything—at least all the major stuff. I focused on my mother once more. "Mom, tell me what happened when our fathers disappeared. *Please.* Has it got something to do with the curse Sherie mentioned before?"

Our three moms joined together again presenting a united front, as though afraid of what was coming next.

I stood firm. I needed to know this. What had happened to my father? Why had my mother spent twenty years alone? Why had I never met him? Or heard his voice? Was even he alive?

When they didn't answer, I persisted. "You all told us that they abandoned you. So, all our lives we've assumed that you had one-night stands with some random assholes who didn't care about you. And those supposed realities drove us to perform the soul mate spell." I glared at each mother, letting the truth of that sink in. "But it seems that was all a lie. You loved them and they loved you. So, our misery was all for nothing. We deserve the truth. So, tell us what happened. Are they still alive? Did they die?"

Ruby gasped, grabbing hold of Tiffany and me as though we were her lifelines or anchor points. "Oh my God, I know who they are! Or were... or whatever."

"Tell me," I said instantly, since my mom didn't seem to want to be honest or more forthcoming.

Ruby's eyes were alight with excitement. "They're the cousins who went missing twenty-two years ago! Jackson and Billy told me about them. Ever since that night, not a single female has been born to the pack. They have all these strong males and no-one to mate with!"

I twisted around to stare at our three mothers, who all looked guilty as hell. I met my mother's gaze defiantly and crossed my arms over my chest. "Sounds like a bloody curse to me."

Continue reading book 2 now:
https://books2read.com/pack-magic

www.ingramcontent.com/pod-product-compliance
Lightning Source LLC
Chambersburg PA
CBHW062309200726
48292CB00004BA/1406